FLOWERS OF ANGER BEAR BITTER FRUIT.

"I'm going to do it Carey. I have to get back at him for Nipper. I don't care what you say, I'm not going to change my mind. I'm not sure yet just exactly how I'm going to do it, but I'll work that out. You'll have to help me. We can set up a watch on his house, you know, time when he goes to bed, when he's away from home, things like that. It'll be fun."

Her face was pleading with me. I wanted to cry for her. I hated what she was doing, but she was still my Annie.

Other Avon Books by
Lynn Hall

GENTLY TOUCH THE MILKWEED	32599	$1.25
THE SIEGE OF SILENT HENRY	34561	$1.25

Available in Avon Camelot editions

NEW DAY FOR DRAGON	30528	$1.25
RIFF, REMEMBER	21899	$ .95
THE SHY ONES	34124	$1.25
STRAY	23473	$ .95
TROUBLEMAKER	26203	$1.25

FLOWERS OF ANGER

LYNN HALL

AVON
PUBLISHERS OF BARD, CAMELOT AND DISCUS BOOKS

AVON BOOKS
A division of
The Hearst Corporation
959 Eighth Avenue
New York, New York 10019

Copyright © 1976 by Lynn Hall
Published by arrangement with Follett Publishing Company.
Library of Congress Catalog Card Number: 76-2235
ISBN: 0-380-01882-9

All rights reserved, which includes the right
to reproduce this book or portions thereof in
any form whatsoever. For information address
Follett Publishing Company
1010 West Washington Boulevard
Chicago, Illinois 60607

First Avon Printing, March, 1978

AVON TRADEMARK REG. U.S. PAT. OFF. AND IN
OTHER COUNTRIES, MARCA REGISTRADA,
HECHO EN U.S.A.

Printed in the U.S.A.

FLOWERS OF ANGER
BECOME BITTER FRUIT.

LYNN HALL was born in a suburb of Chicago and was raised in Des Moines, Iowa. She has always loved dogs and horses and has kept them around her whenever possible. As a child, she was limited to stray dogs, neighbors' horses, and the animals found in library books. But, as an adult, she has owned and shown several horses and has worked with dogs, both as a veterinarian's assistant and a handler on the dog show circuit. Several of her books are about dogs and horses.

For several years Ms. Hall has devoted herself full-time to writing books for young readers. She also works as coordinator and counselor for a local telephone counseling service offering help to troubled young people. Her leisure time is spent reading, playing the piano, or exploring the nearby hills and woodlands on horseback or foot, with a dog or two at her heels.

FLOWERS OF ANGER

ONE

I've been doing some thinking lately about best friends. Everyone has one. At least I hope everyone has one. It would be awful not to. But have you ever stopped to think about how people pick their best friends? Pretty haphazardly, usually, especially when you consider how important that person is to you.

Your best friend knows more about you than your parents do, and generally cares more about you than a boyfriend because, let's face it, boyfriends usually have their ulterior motives. I haven't had one, so far, but I'm not naive. I know how their minds work. So a best friend is an important thing to have.

Most people I know got paired up with their best friends because they were the only ones on their block who were in the same class at school. Or else their mothers were friends, or their older sisters dated their friends' older brothers. No one really puts any sensible thought into choosing a best friend.

Neither did I, though. Ann and I just sort of came together, some time around fifth grade. When I try to remember exactly what it was that I liked about her, the only thing I can come up with, honestly, is that she liked me. I was surprised at first, because in fifth grade I was chunky, and generally people don't like chunky girls that easily. You have to show people that you're nice, friendly, generous, and not dumb in spite of your chunkiness. Then they usually like you, but most people don't give you time for that.

Although I didn't know it then, Ann was very self-conscious about wearing braces. Maybe she chose me because she was sure I wouldn't think I was above her. The braces were only on her bottom teeth, and they didn't really show that much—especially when you added in her good points, her littleness and skinniness and wavy, reddish blond hair.

So maybe our friendship was based on a mutual fear that we couldn't get anybody better. But whatever started it, it's grown over the last five years into something important. We know, now, how important. We found out last summer.

Sarge and I were waiting for Ann to get off work. We waited on the grassy strip behind the root beer stand's parking area, where there was shade for me and grass for Sarge. I sat on the ground and held the ends of the reins, giving Sarge as much grazing room as possible.

He was the ideal horse for me. I can't take any credit for choosing him; my uncle gave him to me after my cousin left for college and didn't need him any more. But if I had been picking out a horse for myself, Sarge would have been it. He was big, mule-colored, kind of ugly because of his Roman nose and one blue eye, but everyone who knew him said Sarge was the most dependable horse they'd ever seen. No bucking or shying or any of those things that Ann used to think were so cute when Nipper did them. Well, luckily, Nipper was her horse and Sarge was mine, and everyone was happy.

Flowers of Anger

It was ten after four before Ann's replacement got there and relieved her of her carhop apron. Ann came running across the sun-glared gravel toward me, holding a Hires bag by its bottom.

"I'm sorry to keep you waiting. I brought some stuff to eat on the way. Let's go."

We laughed at how awkward it was to get her up on Sarge behind my saddle while I sat in front and held the sack. I could feel the two pop cups; I could smell the chili dogs and french fries.

Ann clawed and grappled her way up onto Sarge's back. "I don't know how those women do it in the Westerns," she said. "They just leap up so gracefully behind the handsome stranger and go galloping off into the sunset."

"With long skirts, even. Come on, Sarge, heads up, poor starving baby. You can eat later."

Ann slipped her thumbs through my belt loops and settled herself for the ride. "Ouch . . . ouch . . . ouch," she whispered.

"Saddle pinching you again?"

"Yes, but that's okay."

We never had been able to figure a way to keep her legs from being pinched between the edge of my saddle and the horse. I'd offered several times to let her have the front seat. I was tougher than she was about little pinches and bruises. But she always refused because I was so much heavier, and it would be hard on Sarge's kidneys or liver or whatever it is that I'd be sitting over. So I just tried to hold myself as still as I could in the saddle, to minimize the pinching.

"Through town, or around?" I asked.

"Let's go around. I want to stop at Dad's a minute."

We clopped across the highway, past the drive-in

theater and down into the parking lot of Ann's father's building, a remodeled barn with a sign that said "Hamilton County Veterinary Supplies" across the front. Mr. Johnston saw us through the dusty office window and came outside. He was a huge man, a nice man. I liked him.

"What are you girls up to? I though you were working today, Ann."

"I was, I just got off. Listen, Carey's going to take me out to the farm to get Nipper, and then we're coming back. I thought I'd just tie her out in the yard tonight and save the trip out to get her in the morning, if that's okay with you."

He frowned. "I'm not very crazy about your tying that horse in the yard overnight. She's kind of hard on my lawn, you know."

"She won't be this time, Daddy. I'll tie her where she can't get into anything. We have to be out to the show grounds by eight o'clock in the morning because Carey's in charge of trophies and I'm selling tickets, and I don't want to have to ride her all the way in from the farm plus all the way out to the fairgrounds at that ungodly hour. I promise I'll take care of anything she might do to the lawn."

Mr. Johnston sighed and smiled a little. "Oh, all right, I don't care. Will you be home for supper?"

"Probably not. We might want to mess around awhile out there, and we've got some supper here."

I rattled the sack.

He waved us away. "Go. Die of malnutrition if you want to."

As we rode away Ann gave me a gentle pinch where I flabbed over the top of my jeans. "Oh, yes, we're very malnutrited, aren't we?"

Flowers of Anger

One of the best things about Annie was that back when I was chunky she never mentioned it. She only started kidding me about my size after I got tall enough to be as heavy as I was and not look bad.

Going by the road, it was two miles out to my uncle's farm, where Sarge and Nipper lived. Taking our shortcut, it was almost three. But we preferred the shortcut because it was across country, and we didn't have to worry about cars whooshing by, spooking Nipper, and blowing gravel-road dust all over us. The shortcut was an abandoned railroad bed. The year before, the railroad company had taken up the tracks and ties, leaving us with a lovely raised bridle path. The path curved along the edge of the woods, followed the river, and took us along the back sides of the farms along White Fox Road. Nice of the railroad to do that for us, we thought.

As soon as we were well out of town on the railbed, I hooked the knotted reins over the saddle horn and passed one of the Coke cups back to Ann. The melted ice chips left a watery half inch on top of the Coke; it tasted good anyway, after we had waited so long for it. The sway of Sarge's walk was so familiar a rhythm that we needed no hands for hanging on. Within half a mile our supper sack was emptied, wadded, and thrown, with all due guilt, into the woods.

"We can pick it up on the way back," I said, to appease whatever ecology gods might be watching.

After a while we left the railbed for a narrow path that followed the river. The riverbank dropped off on one side, a rock bluff rose on the other side, leaving only about three or four feet for the path. It used to bother me a lot to ride along there, but I could never say so to Ann. When we came to the narrowest part, where one edge of the path had eroded, Ann said, "Remember that day?"

I shuddered. "Did you have to bring that up?"

The summer before, our saddle club had had a trail ride along this path, and a little boy's horse had spooked at that narrow place and fallen into the river. The boy had been fished out immediately by several of the club members, but he'd been pretty badly banged up, concussion and everything, and he was still in the hospital. For several days after that Ann had lived in terror that her parents would make her sell Nipper. The whole town had been shaken by the accident, and there was quite a bit of talk floating around about how dangerous horses can be for kids. But eventually it blew over, and we were able to relax. Frankly, it wouldn't have bothered me if my parents had said Sarge had to go, but I knew, much better than Ann's parents, even, what it would have done to her if she'd had to give up Nip.

Of course, our families didn't know we were still taking this shortcut out to Uncle Vern's, but with a horse as steady as Sarge it wasn't all that dangerous, or so I kept telling myself while not looking down into the river.

We got past the narrow place and surged up the hill and out onto the camp road, which took us the rest of the way to the clearing at the top of the hill. From the long log dining hall came the sound of thirty Girl Scouts singing "In the Evening by the Moonlight."

"Ah, for the good old days of our childhood," Ann said in her W. C. Fields voice. Together we began singing the dirty version of the song, the one we had sung at Scout camp when the counselors weren't around. Later we'd found out that one of the counselors had made up that version. Then it wasn't so much fun singing it.

As we rode across the broad clearing that held the camp's buildings, four girls wearing camp tee shirts ran toward us. They stopped a respectful distance away and stared at Sarge with shining, pleading eyes. I knew what was coming. Ann's thumb poked me in the side, prodding me toward generosity.

"Could we have a ride?" the boldest girl asked. I stopped Sarge and looked thoughtful. Sometimes Ann and I gave rides and sometimes we didn't, but one of the rules was that you couldn't look too willing to give rides or the kids would just plague you to death. Ann never let anyone ride Nipper because Nip wasn't well enough broken and might be spoiled by bad handling, but Ann was more generous than I was about letting kids ride Sarge. She told me one time that it was the worst feeling she'd ever known, standing down there on the ground, looking up at some older kid sitting smugly on his own horse. She said she used to run off sometimes and cry from the frustration of not being able to ride. I wouldn't have thought it could mean so much to anyone just to get a few minutes' ride down the road and back on somebody's horse, but Ann said it did.

"Oh, I suppose," I said with exaggerated grudgingness, "but you'll have to ride Sarge two at a time. We're in a hurry."

We got off and boosted up the first two girls, and called after them, "Be careful of his mouth, now. Don't jerk him." They grinned as they steered Sarge in and out among the trees at a cautious walk. The second shift got their ride. Then all four girls thanked us, thanked us again, and ran away chattering about how beautiful Sarge was.

Lynn Hall

"You're a sterling human being, Caroline," Ann said as we mounted up.

"Oh, yes."

We skirted the clearing and followed the narrow wooded road out of the campgrounds and through the adjoining public park. Because there were campers and picnickers to watch us, we kicked Sarge into a lope and rocked through the park, our faces solemn, our eyes straight ahead, as though we were so accustomed to the superiority of being on horseback that we didn't even feel their eyes on us.

Through the park and a half mile up the gravel road we loped, and there was Uncle Vern's farm. It was definitely a superior farm; the house was tall and brick, and trimmed with scrollworked wood around the edges; the barn was brick with white frame; white board fences circled the yard and the orchard. Big green letters on the front of the barn said "Valley View Farm." Not too many farms in that part of Iowa had names; but somehow, on Uncle Vern's barn, it didn't seem pretentious. I always got a little proud feeling, coming up his lane and knowing I was related.

We waved to Aunt Mary, who was in the kitchen by the window washing the supper dishes, and she waved a soapy hand back at us. Then we rode on around the barn to the pasture gate.

It was a large, long pasture, nearly eighty acres of open grassland and wooded ravines. Twenty shiny black Angus cows lived there along with Nipper and Sarge. When my two cousins were younger they both raised Angus 4-H calves and showed them at county fairs—beautiful, gleaming blue-black calves with white leather halters. The kids' upstairs bedrooms still held their blue ribbons and browning pictures, cut from the county newspaper, of the cousins and their calves at the fair. I used to be jealous of them till Mom reminded me about the not-so-fun part after the fair, when the calves were sold for slaughter and the cousins had red-rimmed eyes for three days.

"Oh, good, she's close," Ann said. Nipper was grazing with the cattle, not far away. Ann ducked into the barn for her bridle, then started out across the pasture, whistling to Nipper.

Nip raised her head and listened for an instant. Then, when Ann was almost up to her, she spun and galloped away, head and tail up in the air. She was a beautiful animal, a bright bay with black mane and tail and ear rims, and black legs up to the knees. She had no white on her at all, a point that Ann bragged about, although I never understood why.

Nipper was half Arab and half Quarter horse. According to Ann, she had inherited the best qualities of both breeds, including the small, dish-faced head of her Arabian mother. I don't know about all that inheritance stuff; all I know is that on that summer evening Ann's shining red horse galloping against the background of dark green grass, blue sky, and black cattle made an unforgettable picture.

Nipper was playing games. She ran around behind a feed bunker, then lowered her head and grazed until Ann came up and caught her by the halter. I couldn't see them from where I stood, but in just a few minutes Ann was on Nipper's back. The horse danced sideways and did some little bucking half-steps. It would have scared me, especially riding bareback, but Ann loved it. Her face took on a shine when she rode Nip, and especially when Nipper acted up a bit. The horse had a sparkle about her, and when Ann was on her back, Annie sparkled, too.

"Do you care if I work her a little bit before we start back?" Ann called. I shook my head. Riding home in the dark was nothing new for us, and I enjoyed watching Ann and Nipper work out. I held Nipper's reins while Ann saddled her; then I moved farther down the pasture fence to my watching place.

Last fall we had put three oil drums and a row of poles in a flat, open part of the pasture when Ann decided to make a gaming pony out of Nipper. Nip was just a two-year-old then and barely green-broke, but she had shown an eager quickness at barrel racing and pole bending. The next day's show would be Nipper's first time in competition, and Ann's too, so this workout was quite important to her.

My function in these training sessions was to be the "go" shouter. Ann held the dancing Nipper at the starting line till I yelled "Go!" Then they leaped out and whipped around the triangle of oil drums, circling each drum as fast and as closely as possible, or else weaving at top speed through the row of high poles that made up the pole-bending course.

Between my go-shouting duties I just enjoyed the sight of the two of them in motion. They were graceful.

Ann had long dreamed of having her own horse. She had started a fund when she was in the fifth grade. There were baby-sitting jobs, selling loop pot holders and Christmas cards door to door, and anything else Ann could think of to make money. Two years ago the horse fund had finally reached the $300 mark.

While the fund was growing we had spent endless nights sitting on my porch roof trying to decide whether it would be better to buy an older horse or a colt. I kept

Flowers of Anger

voting for an older horse. I didn't think it would be safe for Ann to break a colt herself. But the more I argued, the more she argued. There was nothing like getting a colt and training it yourself, she said. That way you could train it exactly the way you wanted it, and you wouldn't have somebody else's bad habits.

We asked around and found out that Hershal Wilcox, one of the local saddle club members, had a yearling filly that was supposed to be an unusually nice one, sired by a top-winning Quarter stallion from Illinois and out of Hershal's good black Arabian mare. And everyone told us Hershal would sell anything he owned including his wife and kids, if the price was right. We rode our bikes out to Hershal's the next day; there was this bony, unnamed filly, and for Annie, that was it—Nipper.

Nipper was a year and a half old, then, and Ann started right in on training her. That was about the time Ann started running around with this other girl, who also had a horse, and for a while Ann and I didn't see much of each other. It wasn't that she cut me off, it was more my cutting myself off. It seems childish now; it seemed childish even then, but I couldn't help it. I hated knowing that Ann needed me for a friend less than I needed her. I wouldn't have invited a third person to join us, but Ann had.

Then that fall Uncle Vern's youngest son went away to college and there was Sarge—mine for the taking. I took him, and I held off for two days telling Ann that I, too, had a horse. We came back together after that, and as soon as I could make the offer without having it sound like I was trying to buy Ann's friendship, I said she could probably keep her colt at Uncle Vern's, with my horse. After that, in a natural way, there were no more third parties around the edges of Ann and me.

Ann and Nipper finished their workout and we rode back, by the road this time. It was completely dark when we got to the edge of town. We rode along the highway for a few blocks, then up a side street and into the alley. There were three blocks of alley before we got to Ann's backyard. Alleys were more interesting than streets to ride in, because we could look into people's back windows, which to us were more personal than their front ones.

A few yards away from Ann's house we stopped in the shelter of George Greenawalt's garage. Ann got off, crouched behind the trash cans and slowly crawled out, while I held Nipper and watched George's windows till she was beside his strawberry bed. She fingered the plants and squinted to see through the dark.

I saw a shadow at George's kitchen window.

"Look out. Here he comes," I whispered.

She scooted back. "Let's go."

We rode as silently as we could to her backyard, where we could breathe freely and giggle.

While we tied the horses by long ropes to the clothesline posts, I asked, "How does our crop look?"

"Great. They look a little green yet, but another couple of weeks or so and it's going to be strawberry time for us, boy."

I flipped up my stirrup and began working loose the cinch knot. "I wonder if old George ever wonders why he doesn't get more of a strawberry crop than he does, year after year."

"Oh, he's too stupid."

"Annie, do you suppose we're getting too old to be sneaking strawberries out of George's garden?"

Flowers of Anger

We set our saddles inside the garage and walked toward the house on bowed-feeling legs.

She grinned up at me. "I don't feel too old. Do you feel too old?"

"No. I don't feel too old."

I couldn't let her outdo me by too much, even in the department of juvenile behavior. I might lose her again.

TWO

We came in through the kitchen, and our noise made Ann's dad lean out of his chair toward the television set. He waved at us but didn't look away from the screen. We lowered our voices.

"Want something to eat?" Ann whispered.

"I could eat the table, I'm so starved."

We made peanut butter and banana sandwiches and opened a couple of bottles of pop, then took it all into the living room. A commercial was on by then, so we could talk.

"Hi, gals," Ann's mom said. "Did you have a good ride? How did work go, Annie?"

"Fine to both questions." Ann and I curled up on either end of the sofa. Immediately the dogs were up there with us, tromping on our stomachs and staring eagerly at our sandwiches. I didn't mind Sedgewich tromping on me—he was just a little guy, a black poodle—but Old Gold was an overweight yellow Lab, and when he stood on your stomach, he could really mash you.

Ann held her sandwich away from Sedgewich and went on. "Nipper really had a good workout tonight. I couldn't tell for sure without a stopwatch, of course," she said with heavy emphasis, "but I'm sure we've cut a few seconds off our time. Especially on the barrels. Didn't you think so, Care?"

I nodded and gave Old Gold the corner of my sandwich. He wouldn't touch the banana slices, but he was crazy about peanut butter.

The movie resumed. Ann's mother whispered, "This guy here, the older one, is a scientist and the girl is his assistant whom he's in love with, but she doesn't know it, and they're on this little island off the coast of England—"

"Off Scotland," Mr. Johnston said.

"Scotland. Anyway, there are these big blobby things like rocks, only they keep spreading and eating people, and they're getting ready to take over the world."

Mr. Johnston waved her silent, and we all leaned into the story. It got pretty tense there for a while, but then the characters figured out that plain old salt water from the ocean would kill the blobs, and the girl realized that her boss was really the love of her life—and we could all breathe again. Everyone stretched and shifted and made little noises from being so still for so long. The dogs jumped down from the sofa and asked to go out for their ten o'clock run.

Ann's mom got up and opened the door for them. "You didn't say if you had a good day at work." She was in her nurse's uniform and stocking feet. She was short and red-headed like Ann, but she was heavy, at least from the waist down. I liked her a lot.

Ann stared thoughtfully at the ceiling. "I made . . . let's see, $3.85 in tips, which I thought was pretty good for the afternoon shift. It's the night carhops that really make the tips; but even so, if I can average three or four dollars a day in tips for the rest of the summer, that should be enough for a winter's worth of hay *and*," her face got that soft look, and she grinned, "el saddle."

Every time we went to Mason City, which wasn't all that often, we had to stop in at the Corral and visit Ann's saddle. It was in the back room and the tag was marked "sold," but Jim, the owner, wouldn't let Ann take it till it was paid for. He explained very nicely that it wasn't that he didn't trust her; but it was a store policy, especially with kids, because a couple of times kids had bought saddles and got them scratched up and then brought them back, or couldn't pay for them.

Ann was badly in need of a decent saddle. The one she was using was falling apart. But you should have seen the saddle at the Corral—it was just perfect for Ann. Every time I saw her looking at it I wished I had the money to buy it for her. It was black, very plain, with a quilted seat, double rigging, long stirrup covers, and white sheepskin lining. It had a matching breastplate and tie-down, and a black hackamore with braided reins and a white sheepskin noseband. On that shining red and black mare it was going to be gorgeous, especially when you added in little old carrot-top Annie in black frontier pants and white satin shirt with the black piping. I wanted to get her the clothes for her birthday, but as yet Jim and I hadn't figured out a way to get her to try them on, to make sure they fit, without giving away the surprise. They were hanging in the Western Wear corner of the Corral, between the boots and the shelves of Hoof-Flex and fly ointment.

To be honest about it, when we started looking at saddles, I sort of liked the ones with lots of white stitching, red quilted seats, flowers stamped on the stirrup fenders, that sort of thing. But Ann said those sad-

Flowers of Anger

dles looked cheap, and the more I looked at them the cheaper they looked. I hope Ann's still around when I get married so she can help me pick out my wedding dress and furniture and stuff like that. If I ever get married. It looks questionable at this point.

Ann's mother sighed and stepped into her thick white shoes. "Well, I hate to leave this charming company, but—"

Mr. Johnston pulled away from the ten o'clock news. "You want me to drive you?"

"Nah. I need the exercise. Will I see you girls in the morning? When will you need to get up?"

Ann and I looked at each other while we subtracted the time it would take to get dressed and ride out to the fairgrounds from the time we were supposed to be there.

"Six?" Ann said.

I nodded. "I'd think so. We'll be too excited to eat breakfast."

"We'll set the alarm for six o'clock," Ann said, "so we'll probably be gone before you get home."

Mrs. Johnston looked stern and motherly. "Now listen, I don't want you two traipsing out of here without any breakfast. You'll be eating junk out there all day and you're going to need some fuel. Carey, you make Ann eat a good breakfast, will you? And Annie, you make Carey eat. Dad and I'll be out there in plenty of time for your classes. Don't sit up all night talking, now, and Howard, don't forget your pill. Night, all."

The dogs came in as Mrs. Johnston went out.

It gave me a good little glow, her telling Ann to make me eat.

When I first met Ann's family I felt sorry that Mrs.

25

Johnston had to work nights, but after a while I began to realize she loved it. She was head nurse on the eleven-to-seven shift at the hospital—had been for years and years. She told me once that she wouldn't work any other shift if they paid her. That was one of her little jokes that she used all the time, but you had to laugh at them anyway just because she was so nice. She said that during the night shift all the interesting stuff happened—babies being born, guys getting in drunken brawls, and stuff like that. It's such a small hospital that the whole place gets excited every time a baby is born.

My own theory is that she enjoys making waves. Not making trouble, just little waves, like the rest of the family having to arrange their schedules around her sleeping time. She never got a driver's license either, probably for the same reason, because then Mr. Johnston or Mike has to take her places. It's no big hardship for anybody, but I think it makes her feel important. But she's so nice in every other way I don't really hold it against her.

Ann looked at me. "Are you tired?"

I shook my head.

Very carefully, so as not to disturb our houses and hotels, we moved the Monopoly board from the dining room table to the middle of the living room floor. We'd been on this game for several days, off and on. Ann had Boardwalk and Park Place with houses on them, but I had all the rest of that side, all the railroads, and more than half of the rest of the board, so the wealth was pretty evenly divided and we couldn't seem to bankrupt each other.

"Where's Mike?" I asked, not really caring.

"Date," Mr. Johnston said.

Flowers of Anger

"With Sandy?"

"Naturally. Who else?" He stood up and stretched. "If you girls had a bowl of popcorn in front of you, could you be persuaded to eat it?"

We laughed, and he went into the kitchen. There was something he did, making popcorn, that made it come out better than anyone else could make it. He wouldn't tell anyone how he did it. It was his little proud-point.

While we were getting our money stacked out and agreeing that it was time for Ann's brother, Mike, to change girl friends, the phone rang. It was Hershal, who was the head of the committee for the next day's horse show. He wanted to talk to both of us. I got my list of trophy pledges out of the overnight bag I had brought over earlier in the day and read it off to him.

"Western Auto Store, victory figure trophy, Men's Western Pleasure. Super Value, victory figure trophy, Ladies' Western Pleasure. Carl's Feed, same, Ladies' Barrel Racing." And on down the list.

When I finished I gave the phone to Ann so Hershal could tell her where to pick up the cash box and tickets she'd be using at the gate to take admissions. I watched her while I chuted a fistful of popcorn into my mouth. Her face seemed suddenly adult. Did mine, I wondered, when I read Hershal my trophy list? Well, why not? We were sixteen years old, and the saddle club was our first arena of adulthood, if you'll excuse the fancy phrasing. Most of the saddle club members were older than we, of course; young married couples, middle-aged men, several families, and a handful of us high school kids. If we weren't quite accepted on the same level as the adults, at least we were definitely placed higher than the little kids who came to the meetings with their parents. Ann and I had belonged for more than a year by that time, and it seemed to me that we got put on committees just as often as anyone. For the Christmas party they asked Ann to design and make the place cards, so she drew beautiful figures of everyone's horses, exactly right down to their boots, spots, and blazes. No names on them, just the horses, and people went around the table looking for their horses. It was the high point of the whole party.

Ann told me one time that one of her main ambitions in life was to be the first woman president of the Hamilton County Saddle Club, and she could do it, too.

She came back from the phone and was standing, waiting to see what the ten-thirty movie was going to be when a movement at the window caught her eye. I turned to look, too. Nipper was looking in at us from beyond the bridal wreath bushes.

"Oh, shoot, how did she get loose?" Ann said.

Mr. Johnston looked up suspiciously. "Is that horse in the marigolds?"

"No, Daddy, just the bridal wreath, and it's ugly anyhow. Come on, Care, let's go tuck her in."

When we got outside we could see that Nipper's head was bare.

"She must have slipped her halter," Ann said. "I've caught her a couple of times rubbing it off over her ears, against a fence.

"Oh, yes, you're very cute and funny, aren't you, horsetype person? Well, we're not going to play games with you, tootsie. Come on, now."

Automatically Ann and I spread out around Nip. Nipper waited till Ann was just a finger-length from her, then spun away. We had to ease her carefully around the house and into a corner of the garden fence before we could get up to her, but as soon as Ann had her by the forelock, Nip settled right down. She rested her chin on Annie's shoulder and whuffled in her ear and followed along happily while we led her back to where her rope and halter lay in the grass. Sarge watched us with sleepy eyes.

"What are you going to do about her halter?" I asked. "Was it buckled in the last hole?"

"Yeah." Ann picked it up and looked at it. "She has such a little head. She probably needs a pony halter instead of this big old thing. Hold onto her, would you? I'll go punch another hole in it."

She took the halter into the garage and came back several minutes later, after I'd begun to worry about what was taking so long.

"I couldn't find a leather punch or an ice pick or anything like that, but I found a chisel."

"Let me see." I took the halter from her and held it to catch the moonlight. The narrow leather headstrap showed a new wound, a half-inch-wide slit, crossways.

"Uh, oh," I said. "You're always supposed to punch leather, not cut it. This is going to tear."

"No, it won't," she said, slightly miffed. She buckled it onto Nipper's head, and we went back around the house to the front yard to step on all the little cut up places in the grass, from Nipper's hooves. When the divots were all squashed back where they belonged, we sat down on the grass beside the marigolds and went to work on the hoof holes among them.

Do you ever have times when you're suddenly filled with happiness for no apparent reason? I've had maybe three or four times like that, and sitting there with Ann that night was one of them. The feeling is like some sort of revelation that this moment is what being happy means. You know you're going to remember this instant, years later.

The last time I felt that way was a few years earlier, also a summer night, with the same sounds and smells as the night before the horse show. We were thirteen then, I guess. We'd been playing Annie-Annie-Over, throwing a tennis ball over the garage roof, and when it got too dark to see the ball we started playing Hide-and-Seek with a bunch of the younger kids in the neighborhood. Ann and I were too old to play Hide-and-Seek. Maybe that's why it was so much fun, just one more time before we were really too old. No boys our age were around that night, so we didn't have to act sophisticated. I don't understand why, but there had been an almost poignant excitement about hiding behind the bridal wreath that night. I think Ann felt it, too, but we never talked about it.

"There now, no one will ever know," Ann said. We giggled as we stuck broken stems of marigolds into the ground, knowing they weren't going to fool Mr. Johnston. We went inside, decided we didn't feel like Monopoly after all, and went upstairs. Mr. Johnston was involved in the late movie and didn't miss us.

Ann's house is much more my kind of house than my own house is. Hers has big rooms, carved woodwork, carpeting, and an open staircase with a round window at the stair landing. The carpet is purple, which Ann says looks ugly with the tannish walls, but I like it anyway. My house isn't a slum, or anything like that, but it's got hideous flowered linoleum floors, a narrow closed stairway, and an unpainted wooden porch with some rotten boards along the edges. It's close to the

Flowers of Anger

railroad tracks, which is handy for my dad, who works for Rock Island, but it doesn't do a whole lot for my social standing. I said something along those lines to Ann once, and she just said, "What difference does it make what your house is like? It's your parents' house, not yours, and the same for me." I hadn't thought about it that way before, but it's true. After that I didn't worry about what other people thought of 202 Main Street. I just started making plans about the kind of place I wanted to have some day.

We got on our pajamas, turned out the light, couldn't settle down, turned the light on again, brought up the popcorn from downstairs, and worked on our yodeling. We sorted through the country hits albums for the best records with yodeling on them and then played the songs over and over, listening intently to the way the singers' voices made that elusive, intriguing jump. We took turns mimicking them. I was beginning to be able to make my voice do it about half the time, but Ann's voice just faded over the places it was supposed to jump.

Finally, around midnight, our eyes started feeling sandy, and we turned out the light again.

"I'm still too excited to sleep," Ann said, flopping energetically. Her hair was short and coarse and wavy; usually she did nothing with it at night, but that night she made some little curls around the edges and taped them to her face with Scotch tape. Her face was almost solid freckles, and so were her arms and legs. She kind of liked the freckles except that they were such a cliché with red hair. She was a very bony person, actually.

"Hey," I said suddenly in my mother-tone, "didn't you forget something?"

She gave me a dirty look and fished her retainer out of the nightstand drawer. She gave me another dirty look as she worked it into her mouth and hooked it in place.

"Oh, well," I said, "just be glad you're not sleeping with anybody more interesting than me."

"Right. Although at the rate my teeth are going, I'll probably be wearing the wire monster on my wedding night."

We lay still for a while and then she said, "You know what I really worry about, about my wedding night?"

"What?"

"Being ticklish. I have this horrible vision of my husband being very serious and passionate and all that stuff, and accidently touching me in the wrong spot, and I'm going to start giggling and not be able to stop. He'll probably have the marriage annulled right then and there."

With the very lightest brush of my fingertips I touched the bare skin of her side, just above her pajama bottoms. She doubled up, squealing, "Don't, don't. I can't stand it."

Nearly lost in her laughter was the sharp, explosive sound of a gun.

THREE

We froze in position, like a game of statues, I up on my elbow and she curled away from my tickles.

"What was that?"

"Car backfiring, must have been," I said. "Or a blowout?"

We listened for a moment, then Ann kicked up out of bed. "I hope it didn't scare Nipper into bolting and hurting herself."

We padded across the hall and through Mike's room, and looked down into the backyard. It was dark, but we could see Sarge moving restlessly around the clothesline post. Nipper was gone.

"Shoot. She must have broken that halter," Ann said as we ran back for our robes and shoes.

Nipper wasn't in the front yard, nor anywhere in sight up and down the street. We ran around to the backyard. Her rope and empty halter lay in the grass. Through the darkness I could see white around the edges of Sarge's eyes. I had never seen Sarge frightened before; it was oddly upsetting.

Ann came to stand close to me. "Where could she have gone, do you think?"

We stared hard in all directions. Garages, backyards, lilac hedges, trash barrels, all familiar and in place. There was no movement, no horse-sized shadow. George Greenawalt's back porch light was on, that was the only thing.

We both noticed it at the same time. Ann looked at the light, and then she looked up at me and her face went flat and pale. Together we ran—across the yard, up the alley, around the corner of Greenawalts' garage.

George was standing there—a black shape against the yellow porch light. Under his elbow he held a rifle. In the foreground of the scene lay a mound, a horse.

Ann made a small screaming sound. She buried her face in my chest and shook her head, and shook it, and shook it, denying what she saw.

She gasped, "I can't . . . Carey?"

I let go of her and moved toward Nipper's head. Her eyes were open, drying. I lurched back to Ann and shook my head, my eyes streaming.

A voice demanded, "What's happening here?" It was Mr. Johnston. Mike, who had just driven in, was close behind him.

"Mr. Johnston, he shot Nipper. He killed her," I sobbed. I couldn't let go of Annie, nor she of me.

Mr. Johnston turned to face George, who was coming slowly across the yard, no longer carrying the rifle. "What's happening here, Greenawalt?"

In the twanging tension I almost giggled at Mr. Johnston's western-movie tone.

George was a small man, middle-aged, even more colorless that night than usual. "Listen, Howard, I didn't intend to kill it, but it was ruining my gardens. My roses."

Mr. Johnston swelled with anger. "That was my girl's pet. You had no right in the world to shoot my girl's pet."

Flowers of Anger

George stiffened. "I was within my legal rights. The animal was on my property. Doing damage. I was within my rights."

The two men stared at each other, then broke loose. Mike knelt beside Nipper's neck and felt her, looking for a pulse, I supposed. He rose and shook his head.

Mr. Johnston turned toward home, motioning to Mike and Ann to follow. "We'll be seeing about this, Greenawalt," he said.

Over the top of Ann's head I stared all of my hate into George Greenawalt's eyes. I let go of Ann and walked over to him. I couldn't speak. I had never hated anyone before. When my voice finally came out, it shook. "Why did you kill her horse?"

He didn't answer.

"Why did you kill her horse!"

Then Mike's hand was on my arm, turning me toward home. I think I punched Mike; I'm not sure. He never said anything about it. When we got home they called Ann's mother, and she came home from work and held Ann and they cried together for a few minutes. I sat on the floor in the corner and held on to the dogs. Finally, since there seemed nothing to say, we all went to bed and Mrs. Johnston went back to the hospital.

We lay in bed, Ann and I, separately, silently. I tried to think what I could say that would make her feel less terrible, but there wasn't anything. She curled up with her back to me and a wad of wet Kleenexes in her fist. All I could do was pet her head and say, "I know. I know."

We were still awake when the sky began graying up. I didn't want to go to the show, but Annie insisted there was nothing I could do for her, and she said it was no use letting the saddle club down; somebody was going to have to take tickets. So I put on my new bone-white Levi's and green shirt with the pearl buttons, and the cowboy boots I'd bought because Ann had a pair. I drank some milk and made two pieces of toast but only ate one. Then I went out and got Sarge saddled. I kissed his neck. I don't usually do things like that.

The truck from the rendering plant was coming up the alley as I rode away, coming to haul Nipper away. Coming to make her into glue and dog food.

I tried my best not to think about Nip and Annie as I rode across town, out on Eighth Street till it became a gravel road, then on to the county fairgrounds. Half a dozen trucks and horse trailers were there already— Hershal's red and white stock truck and the Paris's green horse trailer and several others from the club. People were hooking up the loudspeaker system at the ring entrance, and an open-sided refreshment van was selling coffee and rolls. In the field behind the ring, kids were riding around, showing off.

I found Hershal bending over the entry table, at ringside, arguing over class sheets with Mrs. Paris. Hershal was a big guy with black, wavy hair, and very red cheeks. He had a Missouri accent. He always struck me as a sort of poor man's movie hero type. He was a nice enough guy, but he had an obnoxious habit of patting fannies when he'd had a few beers.

He looked up at me. "Hi, kiddo. Where's Ann? I've got her cash box and tickets here. She better be—"

"Ann's not coming, Hersh. Her horse got killed last night. I'll sell tickets if you want me to."

Flowers of Anger

He straightened up, shocked. "Got killed? Nipper? How?"

I made my voice bitter so I wouldn't start bawling again. "Our illustrious county clerk shot her. Ann had her in the backyard last night, so we could get over here early, and I guess Nipper broke her halter and wandered over there, in his yard, and messed up his garden. So he shot her. I tell you, Hersh, I never wanted to kill anybody before in my life, but boy—"

"Oh, no," Hershal said. "Not that nice little mare. God. And after all the work and training that little gal put into her. How awful!" He shook his head. "Well, listen, time's kinda short here this morning. You want to take the tickets, then? A dollar for adults, fifty cents for kids under twelve, use your own judgment, and you can take that card table over there, that chair, and try to find yourself some shady place. And listen, you tell Annie I got a couple of dandy colts out to my place. I wasn't going to sell them, but you tell her to come on out and if she wants one she can just take her pick, and pay me when she can."

"Thanks, Hersh. I'll tell her."

I started to walk away, but he called after me, "Carey?" I turned. "You tell that little girl she better get herself another horse just as quick as she can. I've been through it and I know. It's the only way to get over losing one."

I nodded. I agreed with his philosophy, but I had a feeling it was going to be a little while before Ann could turn to another horse.

I worked the gate all morning, taking admissions and telling people the best places to park their cars. Then one of the Paris kids came and took over for me while

Lynn Hall

I rode Sarge in the Ladies' Western Pleasure Class. We got eighth place in a class of eight, about what I'd expected. The show was over by about six o'clock but then we had to clean up all the pop cups, beer cans, and trash—which took forever—and I helped unstring the announcer's public address stuff, the mike and the loudspeakers that hung from light poles around the ring.

When practically everyone had left and I was tightening Sarge's cinch and dreading the long, dark ride out to Uncle Vern's, Hershal came over, offered to truck Sarge to the farm for me, and give me a lift home. At that point I was so tired I could have kissed his boots for the offer.

We unloaded Sarge at the farm. Hersh insisted on tossing my bike into the truck and taking me back to town. We made a supper stop at the Shamrock, which is where my mom works. It's sort of a truck stop on the highway at the edge of town, a pretty nice place—clean, anyway—and the food is good. When we were in junior high, Annie and I used to get a big thrill out of hanging around the Shamrock and flirting with the truck drivers. At least we thought we were flirting; I don't think any of them took us seriously, thank God. Of course, when Mom started working there, that was the end of that. But it is a nice place. It's got pine paneling and almost all of my favorite songs on the jukebox.

The Shamrock was almost empty when Hersh and I went in. Nine o'clock on a Sunday night isn't one of their rush times. Mom was in the kitchen, but she saw me through the little window and came out. I wasn't too sure she was going to like my running around at night alone with Hershal. She knew his reputation as a fanny-patter. What she didn't know was that I had al-

Flowers of Anger

ready settled that little matter with Hersh a long time ago, when he first made a pass at me, one night after saddle club meeting. I told him in no uncertain terms that I wasn't interested in messing around, that I wanted him for a friend but that we couldn't be friends if I had to keep defending myself from him all the time. He thought about it for about half a minute and said, "That makes sense," and promptly went back to talking horses. He and I have been pretty good friends ever since. But as I say, Mom didn't know about all that.

She didn't say anything, though, when she came out of the kitchen. She kind of smiled at Hersh, then looked at me sadly, with her head tilted, and said, "Honey, I'm so sorry about Annie's horse."

Hersh and I took stools at the counter, and Mom pulled her own little stool out from under her side of the counter so she could get off her feet while we talked. My mom is a pretty good old girl. If I were seeing her for the first time I'd have to call her a homely woman, long face, big teeth, and stuff like that. But we get along pretty well.

"What happened, anyway?" she asked. "You were right there. Just about everybody that's been in here today has been talking about it, but nobody had any details, just that George Greenawalt shot her horse."

I told her everything. By then, it was just about like reciting a poem for English class; I'd told the story so many times at the horse show. While I was telling it, Hersh quietly stuck his head in the kitchen and ordered us fries and roast beef sandwiches, and he helped himself to a couple of cups of coffee from behind the counter. Mom started to get the stuff, but he motioned her away. When the sandwiches were ready, old fat

Ada, the cook, came out and sat with us. She is some sort of shirttail relative of mine, but I'm not sure what the connection is. She's nice, if you don't have to smell her breath.

Mom said, "I wonder what's going to happen now. Is Howard going to sue George, or anything, do you think?"

I shook my head. "I don't have any idea. All we talked about last night was just, well, trying to get Ann calmed down. Could they sue him?"

Ada joined in. "They'd ought to, that's for sure. A man can't just go around shooting a child's pet like that, and be allowed to get away with it. What was he doing with a gun, in town, anyhow, I'd like to know. It just makes me so mad I could chew horseshoes and spit nails."

Hershal squirted a stream of ketchup over his french fries and sandwich, then did the same for mine. "I don't know just what the legalities of the situation would be," he said slowly. "Naturally we all feel the same about his shooting Nipper, but, legal-wise, he might have been within his limits. The horse was on his property and doing damage." He raised his hands to ward off my furious stare. "Now, sis, I'm just trying to look at it from a legal standpoint. For myself, I'd like to, well, I won't say in front of you ladies what I'd like to do to George Greenawalt. I just hope Ann's daddy takes him to court."

"I'll tell you one thing," Mom said, "it's going to be a cold day down under when that man gets re-elected, that's for sure. I don't expect there's one person in this town that would go along with what he did, legal or not."

Flowers of Anger

Ada leaned in close and I buried my nose in my coffee cup's steam. "You know what they used to say about George and those cat traps, don't you? I always did believe it, and now I *really* believe it."

"What was that?" Hersh asked. He lived out in the country and didn't always get in on the town gossip.

I said, "Oh, they've been saying George used to have a cat trap set all the time, out in his garden, and if some neighbor's cat came in there he'd catch it and kill it."

"Was it true?"

"I don't know," I said, shrugging. "But I know Ann said there were several times when really nice pet cats just disappeared, and they weren't the kind of cats that would be likely to run away. There was that beautiful gray Persian cat that Ann's next-door neighbors had had for years, and I remember one that some little kids had, it was a darling little calico kitten."

"Why would he want to kill cats?" Mom asked.

"Because he loves birds," I said bitterly. "He was always talking about the cats killing his stupid cardinals. Just like his killing Nipper because he loves his roses so much. It doesn't make sense to me, that a person can love birds and flowers, and at the same time be cruel enough to kill a kitten or a beautiful horse."

We all shook our heads and got quiet.

I had to watch the younger kids the next morning, so it was after lunch before I could get over to Ann's house. She was in her room, still in her pajamas, sitting on the bed listening to her Eddie Arnold album.

"Aren't you going to work?" I asked. She was due at the root beer stand in an hour.

She looked up at me with puffy eyes. "Hi, Care.

No, I called and told them I wouldn't be working any more."

"What do you mean, not working any more? You're quitting your job, that half the girls in school tried to get? Why?" I already knew why.

"Because. Why not? What's the point in working? The only reason I needed that job was to pay for the saddle," her voice caught, "and buy hay for this winter. Not much point in that now," she said bitterly.

"Oh, come on, Annie." I sat down beside her. My instinct was to pick up her hand and hold it, but we could only touch each other in moments of crisis or joy, when we weren't noticing what we were doing. Hugging or holding hands any other time might mean we weren't normal. So I didn't take her hand, although I think maybe she needed me to. I gave her a light punch that didn't quite connect.

"Come on. Call him back and tell him you changed your mind. I don't think you should quit your job. You'll need the money to get—" I hesitated—"a new horse." I hadn't meant to bring it up so soon.

She just shook her head.

"Well, look. School clothes, then. Look at all the clothes you could buy with that money."

Bad argument. It was like saying Nipper could be replaced by a bunch of new clothes. I went on, quickly, "But I really think you're wrong about not wanting to get another horse. Okay, maybe it's too soon to be talking about it, but please, Annie, think about it." My voice got softer than I meant it to.

She shook her head again. "It wouldn't be Nip."

"Of course it wouldn't. It would be a whole new personality. A whole new set of challenges. Look at all you learned about horse training from Nipper. You

Flowers of Anger

could get another yearling colt and probably do an even better job with it than you did with Nip, and you know all the compliments you got from everybody at saddle club about the way you broke Nipper."

She didn't say anything, so I went on. "I have a message for you from Hersh. He says to tell you he has two very nice colts out at his place, and he wasn't going to sell them to anyone because they're such good ones he wanted to keep them for himself; but he said you could have whichever one you wanted and just pay for it when you got the money. He told me all about them. One is a yearling filly that looks like she's going to be a blue roan. She's out of that nice black mare of his that you always liked, and the sire is a registered Tennessee Walker. And the other colt is a sorrel gelding Quarter horse, with papers and everything, and Hershal says he's just as flashy as can be."

She shook her head angrily. "No, Carey, I mean it. I don't want to even hear about another horse. Frankly, all I want to do at this point is to figure out some way of murdering George Greenawalt."

"I think murder is frowned on in this state."

She allowed a tight half-smile to slip past her defenses, and happiness broke all over my face. But then she said, "No, don't make me smile. I'm not ready to be jollied out of it. Care, I'm serious about this. We've got to think of some way to make him pay for what he did to Nipper. I want to hurt that man."

"Me, too." I remembered the way I felt, standing there staring into George's eyes while Ann bawled on my chest and her beautiful Nipper lay stiffening on the ground beside us. I had never thought of myself as a vengeful person before, nor Annie, for that matter, but then nothing really bad had ever been done to either of us until then.

"Is your dad going to sue him?" I asked. "They were talking about it at the show yesterday. You were missed, by the way, and all kinds of people were asking me about what had happened. Everyone was very nice and felt sorry."

Ann sniffed. "I think Daddy is going to ask his lawyer about it. He said something last night about at least checking into it."

"Good. We'll get our revenge fair and square, then."

I risked a pat on her arm. Ann sniffed again and looked doubtful.

FOUR

I was in the middle of a huge ironing when Ann came over the next afternoon. You'd think it would be impossible to accumulate three baskets of ironing in just one week in this age of permanent press, but with a big family like ours it can be done. I have two younger sisters and four younger brothers. I know one thing for sure; I'm not going to have a big family. Preferably no children at all. Maybe even no husband, I haven't decided about that yet. But one of my favorite daydreams, especially in the middle of a big ironing, is to live absolutely alone.

No, I guess that was one daydream I borrowed from Ann. Deep down I know I'm the kind who has to have people around. It's just ironing that makes me wish I lived alone.

Later when Ann came over I was through with the shirts and blouses and was down to the flat stuff. She came into the dining area where I was ironing, slid a pile of boys' underwear out of her way, and sat down sideways to the table. Immediately Catface, our poor old beat-up yellow tom, jumped into her lap, kneaded a nest, and curled down, purring. I was surprised to see Ann in a dress on a summer afternoon.

"What's up?" I asked.

"We have an appointment at the lawyer's this afternoon," she said. "Daddy and I. Can you come?"

I was pleased, as I always was when she showed some sign of needing me. "Yeah, I guess. How come you want me to go along?"

She shrugged. "Moral support. A friend in court. Hey, that rhymes. I don't know, I just want you to come along. Do you have to baby-sit this afternoon or anything?"

"No, Marcy's here." She's the next oldest. "What time are we supposed to be there? And where?"

"In an hour, at Lister and Lister's, up over the bank. Daddy's going to meet us there."

I went into high gear with the iron and only did one side of the pillowcase. It pleased me that Ann was looking and sounding more alive than she had the day before. Her face still had a kind of stiffness about it, but at least it didn't look weepy.

"I tried all morning to call you," Ann said, "but your line was busy. So I thought I'd just come and get you."

"Jerry was on the phone, and then Marcy was on the phone, and then Jerry was on the phone, and on and on. What should I wear?"

"A skirt or dress, I guess. You're probably not supposed to wear shorts to a lawyer's office. Wear that striped outfit, why don't you. Here, I'll finish the ironing, and you can get ready."

"You're on. Of course, you realize you're the only person in the world for whom I would put on panty hose and a skirt in June. Not to mention shoes."

"I appreciate your sacrifice. Sorry, Catface, the lap has to stand up now."

Flowers of Anger

We bantered, but it was automatic. Both of us were tense about what the lawyer was going to say.

We got to Lister and Lister's office fifteen minutes early, in spite of walking slowly. A narrow brown stairway flanking the First State Bank led us up; then we went through a frosted door into the outer office. I'd been in that building many times to see my dentist, who has his office at the other end of the hall, but I'd never been inside one of the lawyers' offices on that floor. Lister and Lister's office was nice, but small. Definitely a comedown from lawyers' offices on television. And the receptionist was middle-aged. She smiled and motioned us to the chairs and magazines.

Even though neither of us had any reason to feel nervous, it was a relief when Ann's dad came through the frosted door, looking big, cheerful, and comfortable. Almost immediately we were shown into the inner office, where Mr. Lister rose from behind his desk and shook hands all around, even with me. He didn't seem surprised at my being there, nor did he ask me to wait outside, as I'd been afraid he might. That would have been embarrassing as well as frustrating. I didn't want to miss any of this.

"Now then," Mr. Lister said, "Howard, what's the problem?" He looked a little bit like Jimmy Stewart but had a deeper voice. I decided I liked him.

Mr. Johnston took a big breath and settled snugly into his chair. "Well, as you know, we had some trouble last Saturday night with Ann's horse. Briefly, what happened was that Ann had ridden the horse into town and tied her up in our backyard overnight, because she had to be out at the fairgrounds early the next morning for the saddle club horse show. So. The horse broke her halter around—I don't know—midnight or so, and went wandering off. She ended up in George Greenawalt's backyard, evidently did a little damage to his garden, and he shot the horse, killed her. We all got down there within just a few minutes after the shot, Ann, me, Carey here, who was staying the night at our house, and my son Mike, who had just gotten home from a date. There were some neighbors that came out, too, Petersons, Mrs. Hempel, and a few others; I'm not sure just who."

"And George admitted to shooting the horse?"

"Lord, yes. There was no question about that. The girls saw him with the gun under his arm, but he put it down when I got there. First, he said he'd only meant to scare Nipper off, that he didn't mean to kill her. But then he started in about how he was within his rights, she was on his private property, all that sort of thing."

Mr. Lister made notes on a scratch pad and said, "Um hm? Um hm?"

Ann's father went on. "What I want to know, Jack, is whether he was within his legal rights and if not, can we do something about it? Aside from the fact that the horse was my girl's pet, it was a good horse, a good deal more valuable than whatever damage she might have done to his yard."

Mr. Lister looked at Ann. "What was the value of the horse, would you say, Ann?"

I knew what Ann was thinking. I could read the pain behind her eyes, the answer she wanted to give, about the impossibility of putting a money price on the life of something you love. But she answered sensibly, and I was proud of her.

"I paid two hundred and seventy-five dollars for her, but she was just a yearling then, not even green-broke. I broke her myself," her voice wavered, "and I was training her as a gaming horse, you know, barrel racing and all that. She was very good at it, and a good young gaming horse, especially with her breeding and her looks, would probably bring four, five hundred dollars around here. Maybe more, if she had a lot of wins and trophies already."

Mr. Lister considered for a moment, then made another notation. "Would you say four hundred would be a reasonable value, then, for this particular horse as she stood?"

Ann looked at her father, and at me. We both nodded slightly. "Yes, about that."

"Well, Howard," Mr. Lister tipped way back in his chair and frowned and hit his teeth with his pen, "George did not have any legal right to kill the animal. No. In this state we have laws of distraint, you see, which means holding an animal which has strayed onto your property, holding it for a certain length of time until the owner claims it. If there is damage to the property and the owner of the strayed animal refuses to pay the damages, then the property owner can sell the animal and keep enough money to pay for the damages to his property. But, no, the property owner has no right to kill the animal."

We all breathed and looked at each other.

Mr. Lister got down some huge books on Iowa law and read aloud some of the long, confusing passages about distraint laws, fencing laws, boundary laws, livestock laws.

Finally Mr. Johnston got him back on the subject. "Then we could sue George?"

"Yes, certainly. I would say he would certainly be liable for the value of the horse, less whatever damage might have been done to his property, which shouldn't amount to much. But I doubt it would go to court. I don't know who George's attorney is, if he even has one, but I'd imagine whoever he got would advise him to settle out of court. I'll go ahead with it if you'd like."

Mr. Johnston looked at Ann and raised his eyebrows, asking.

Her voice was small but hard. "Yes. Sue him. Make it go to court, so he'll have to stand up in front of everybody and tell people what a son-of-a-bitch he is."

"Ann!" Her dad was shocked. I don't suppose anyone but me had ever heard Annie swear before.

"Well, I mean it. That's all very well for him to pay for Nipper, but—it doesn't really help." Her voice trailed away at the end.

We left Mr. Lister's office and filed back down the stairs and out onto the sidewalk. We were in the middle of the three blocks of downtown. The office is on the block with the best stores. The block to the east has mostly taverns and junky places, like the plumbing supply place and Harley's Electric; and the block to the west has a lot of dusty antique stores, the movie theater, which only runs three nights a week, and the library, which used to be the Salvation Army building.

"Can I give you girls a lift somewhere?" Mr. Johnston asked.

"No, that's okay, we'll walk," Ann said. She forgot to thank him, so I did, under my breath. He gave me a little wink.

We were feeling a bit up in the air, or at least I was, charged up, unready to go home, too dressed up to want to go home. It seemed funny not to be out in the country, riding, that afternoon. I felt as though we should be over at the Girl Scout camp giving rides on

Flowers of Anger

Sarge, or out in the back pasture at Uncle Vern's looking for wild raspberry bushes, or riding the horses back and forth across the water splash in the park, getting our legs and feet wet and showing off in front of the campers.

We set out aimlessly, meandering up one side of the block and down the other. We tried on a couple of swim suits in Anthony's, leafed through the slacks and blouse racks in Wards, poked around the shoe pyramid in the back part of Modern Fashion, and automatically made fun of the cheap-looking negligee sets in the window of Mode-O-Day. We picked out our engagement rings in the window of the jewelry store, but without much spirit.

"Want a root beer float?" I asked. "I'm buying."

We went to our booth at the very back of the Elite Cafe. It felt like home. The summer before we had been on a berry-berry sundae kick. That's raspberry ice cream with strawberry topping. This year it was root beer floats. I loved the foam, with the little scum of brown on it.

"Well," I said, looking quizzically at Ann. We had avoided talking about it all through our window-shopping, waiting, I suppose, till we were in our booth, quiet and seated.

"Well?" she shot back.

I shugged. "It looks like you're probably going to win it, from what he said."

"Win what, Nipper back alive again?"

I looked down into my brown scum. "The money, anyway, Andy." I hadn't called her Andy since sixth grade. "I know, I know. It's not the same as having Nip back, but it's the next best thing. You can buy a new horse. One of Hershal's colts, maybe. And probably have enough left over to pay off your saddle at the Corral."

She just shook her head.

"But why not? What more do you want? Blood? I'm sorry. Bad choice of words. But what more *do* you want out of Greenawalt?"

"I don't just want them to settle it out of court," Ann said grimly. "That wouldn't be enough. That would be just money. I want it to be a regular trial, with stories in the newspaper and everything."

When she met my eyes, her stare had a hard sparkle to it. I was glad to see her showing more life than she had since the shooting, and yet I found myself wishing it was the prospect of a new colt that made her eyes gleam like that, rather than the prospect of revenge.

Without thinking I said, "I never knew you to be a vindictive person before."

Her face hardened. Ann didn't like criticism. "Why should you? What have I ever had to be vindictive about, before? Either one of us, for that matter. And how do you know how you'd react if somebody did something awful to you?"

"Right."

She had a point. Nothing really bad had ever happened to either of us before, no deaths in our immediate families, no divorced parents or serious illnesses, nothing to test what we were made of.

"Anyway," I went on, "I'm not saying this as a criticism, or anything like that, but I really do think you should keep your job at the root beer stand. And I really honestly think you should get another horse."

She shook her head, and we spooned our fizzy ice cream globs in silence for several minutes.

Finally I said, "Look. I just had an idea. Why don't

Flowers of Anger

I see if your job is still open, and if it is, I'll take it myself, just to keep the owner from hiring someone else. Then any time you decide you want it back, you can have it, okay?"

She thought for a moment, then her face softened into a smile. "Okay, if you want to, but don't count on my wanting it back. That's nice of you to think of it. You're not as rotten as people say you are."

We grinned at each other, and I began to feel as though things were going to get better.

As soon as I got home I called the owner of the root beer stand and asked him if Ann's job was still open. "Yes," he said, "it sure is." He said he'd hired a girl; she worked one day and quit because it was harder work than she thought it was going to be, so if I wanted the job, it was mine. When I explained that I wanted it just until Ann got to feeling better and would want it back, he said he didn't care which one of us worked, just so the shifts were covered, and just so I was neat and pleasant to the customers. It would be the night shift instead of days, he said, four or five nights a week, from four to ten o'clock with about a half-hour of clean-up work after ten o'clock, and could I start right away? I said, you bet.

I got out of the intensely aggravating nylons I was still wearing, and into denim shorts, a blue gingham shirt, and my best navy blue tennis shoes, and set out for my first day—night, actually—on my first job.

For the first couple of blocks of the walk to the root beer stand I was nervous about it. But then I got to thinking, what did I have to be scared about? I didn't know any less about carhopping than any other new girl they'd had, and I figured I was smarter than a good many they'd hired.

And the more I thought of it, the more important it became that I should make a success of something Ann had succeeded at but failed to stay with. It had something to do with the balance between Ann and me. We both got good grades at school, but Annie got them almost without studying. She had better taste in clothes than I, her hair usually looked neater than mine, and she had already had a couple of dates, more or less. She was planning to go to college; I was planning to get a job after high school. It wasn't that there was an open sense of competition between us, but every once in a while I felt compelled to excel in something over her for the sake of keeping the balance between us. If she had more of a flair for things, then my strength lay in what I liked to think of as my—well—steadfastness. She was a starter; I was a finisher.

Actually, the job turned out to be much easier than I had expected. I already knew the menu by heart, from having spent so many summers eating there, so it was just a matter of learning a few abbreviations for things like hamburgers with everything but onions and a large root beer to go. Since this was strictly an economy outfit, the only uniforms were short canvas aprons with change pockets in them. All I had to do was stick the menu card on the windshield, smile, return to take the order, pass it through the window to the cook, take the tray back to the car, say, "Would you roll up your window a little, please?" and collect the money. After the first hour I felt completely at ease and quite pleased with myself.

Flowers of Anger

I had only two coworkers, Chuck, the cook, and Marsha Smith, the other carhop. Chuck was very nice. He was married to the older sister of one of the girls in my class, so I knew him slightly. He was going to college, had been in the service, and was a sweet looking man because of his huge nose. There is something endearing about a man with a big nose. Chuck was pleasant and patient with me even when we got busy. I decided I would probably have a crush on him before long.

Not that it ever did me any good to have crushes. No one ever knew about them except Ann.

Marsha was nice to me, too. She was a year behind me in school, but we had been in the same phys. ed. class and played on the same softball team, so we were already on a friendly basis. She showed me everything I needed to know and complimented me on how fast I learned, which, of course, made me feel good. I'd always liked Marsha, although she was one of those people you just never noticed much. I was probably one that others never noticed much, too, come to think of it.

Just before closing time a car pulled in and parked on my half of the territory. I started toward it but stopped when I saw the driver. I backed up and whispered to Marsha, "Hey, would you mind getting that car for me?" Then I eased around the corner of the building and looked at him through the pass-through window.

It was George Greenawalt.

I looked at him, and I looked at my feelings, looking at him. I felt churned, remembering the scene in his backyard Saturday night, but I no longer wanted to kill him or do anything else drastic to him.

55

Ann was sitting home, mourning the death of her beloved horse, and there I was, her best friend, looking right at the guy and feeling nothing more violent than dislike and distaste.

What kind of a best friend was I?

I stared at George and remembered Nipper lying there, and in a minute or two the hate began to boil.

FIVE

The best word I can think of to describe the next couple of weeks is *blah*. The job was fun, and I was making six or seven dollars a night in tips, besides the salary, so that was nice, but it was only four nights a week. The rest of the time was empty and heavy.

At first I was going over to Ann's every day, midmorning or so, as soon as all the kids were dressed and they had had their breakfast, and Mom and I had had our coffee and what's-new-with-you-since-yesterday talk over the toast crumbs and stray Cheerios on the kitchen table. But Ann was still so far down she didn't seem to care whether I came over or not.

She'd gotten started watching soap operas on television, so we could only talk during the commercials. You know, it's very hard to say to someone, "Look, I care about you. I hurt for you. Please try not to grieve so hard. Try to make a start at putting things back together. Life goes on," and so forth, to a background chorus of people who took the wrong kind of laxative.

We always had to be quiet, too, because Ann's mom would be asleep, so I couldn't get really mad at Ann. I was beginning to feel more and more like putting a foot through the television screen to get her attention.

After a week or so I quit going over there. I told

myself, if she wants to turn off the world, fine, but it's no reason for me to quit living, too, just to keep her company.

But I ached for her.

I went out to Uncle Vern's about every other day, and I'd walk out in the pasture and visit with Sarge for a while, maybe get on him and sit there making braids in his mane and letting him move me around the pasture a step at a time while he grazed. Once I got ambitious and did a French braid down the top of his tail, but he accidentally kicked my foot, aiming at a fly, and it hurt like heck through my tennis shoes, which had holes in the sides anyhow, so that was the end of the tail braid.

I usually ended up in the house, where it was nice and cool. Aunt Mary was always so glad to have somebody to talk to that she made me feel good.

One night, when we weren't very busy at the root beer stand, Marsha asked me if I wanted to go to the show with her the next night. Neither of us had to work that night, and it was a show I wanted to see. In fact, before she mentioned it, I was more than half planning to go. I opened my mouth to say sure, but I didn't say it.

"Um, I can't tomorrow night, but thanks anyway." I sort of looked to the side when I said it, and I had the feeling she knew I was lying. But she was nice about it. When closing time came I told her I'd do the clean-up if she wanted to go on home. She kind of smiled, as though she knew I was trying to make up for not wanting to go to the show with her.

After she left, Chuck and I started the clean-up routine, putting the ketchup and mustard and relish back in the big jars and into the walk-in refrigerator, wash-

Flowers of Anger

ing out the stainless steel wells, filling the salt shakers, checking out the cash register, washing down all the counter tops, and scrubbing the grill.

"Chuck, do you ever do anything stupid?" I asked as I bore down, hard, on the grill with the emery scrubber.

He just laughed and said, "Why? What stupid thing did you do?"

"Oh, it was just dumb. Marsha asked me if I wanted to go to the show with her tomorrow night and I said I couldn't, but I could if I wanted to, and furthermore I really want to see that show, and tomorrow would be the only night I could go, and now I can't because if she's there and sees me . . ."

One nice thing about Chuck is that he always knows when you're kidding around and when you're serious about something, even though you may sound like you're kidding around.

He said, "So why didn't you want to go, when she asked you? Or did you just not want to go with her?"

I thought about it while I worked away at a stubborn spot of burned grease. "I didn't want to go with her. But I don't know why not, Chuck. I like Marsha, and I don't like to go to movies alone, because then there's nobody to laugh with at the funny parts. Ann and I always . . ." I stopped, not really knowing what I'd intended to say.

"Maybe you didn't feel right about going to the show with anybody but Ann, do you suppose?"

Chuck didn't know Ann too well, since they'd only worked together a few times, but he knew she and I had run around together for years and that we were generally thought of as a set around town. It was always "Ann and Carey" this, and "Carey and Ann" that.

I thought about what he said. "That's possible," I said slowly, "but it doesn't make sense, really. She's just my girl friend. It's not like I was dating a boy and another boy asked me out."

"Okay, go back in your mind and try to remember your exact thoughts and feelings in that split second, when Marsha asked you and you said no. What exactly was going through your mind?"

Chuck was studying psychology, and sometimes I think he practiced on me.

I closed my eyes. What thoughts had gone through my head? Wanting to go to the show, being pleased that Marsha wanted my company, a flash of guilt for being pleased, a flash of imagining how I would feel if Ann went to the show with somebody else.

That was it, then. I didn't want to hurt Ann's feelings by doing something with Marsha. I couldn't decide whether it was noble of me, or just stupid and self-destructive.

The next Tuesday night was saddle club night. I didn't ask Ann ahead of time whether or not she was planning to go for fear she'd just make up some excuse. By that time she'd been moping for so long I was beginning to get worried about her. There was something about her skin and her eyes that didn't look very good. I figured she needed a night out with real live people, and I was determined that she was going to go.

I got dressed up in my best off-white Levi's, made my usual three-bean salad for the pot-luck supper, and set off for Ann's house with a good hour to spare. Mom didn't have to work that night, so I got her car, which

Flowers of Anger

was nice, because nine blocks is too far to walk balancing a drippy casserole and carrying a plate and silverware.

Ann's mom was in the kitchen when I knocked at the back door. She waved me in and went on with her work. She was antiquing a picture frame on some newspapers on the kitchen table. "Ann's upstairs," she said. "How've you been?"

"Fine, thanks. Um, is she planning to go to saddle club tonight?"

She frowned up at me. "Is that tonight? She didn't say anything about it. See if you can't talk her into it, though, Carey. She's as full of fun as a crutch these days. She needs to get out."

I started through the kitchen.

"Carey? Is it pot-luck?"

"Yeah."

Mrs. Johnston stared at the ceiling, then said, "I'll fix up a relish tray that she can take, so don't let her wiggle out of it on that excuse, okay?"

I saluted and went upstairs.

Ann was lying across her bed, reading.

"Come on, up and at 'em," I said cheerfully. "This is saddle club night, or did you forget? Your mom is fixing a relish tray for you to take, so you've got no excuse for not going."

"Hi," she said.

"Hi. Now cut the formalities and get dressed. Wear your, let me see, um, wear your yellow polka-dotty slacks thing."

She shut her book and sat up, a move in the right direction, I thought. She looked as though she had the kind of headache you get from too much lying around indoors.

"I really don't feel like going to saddle club."

"You'll feel like it after you get there. Come on. Do it as a favor to me, will you? And before you say no, when was the last time I asked you for a favor, and how many times have I done stuff for you that I didn't feel like doing?"

She thought for a minute, then smiled. "Okay, if you're going to blackmail me. I'll go, but I won't enjoy myself. Fair enough?"

I was elated at the return of even a spark of her usual humor, and I took it as another good sign when she put on the yellow slacks set. She knew very well she looked darling in it. Her mother gave me a congratulatory pat on the back as we went out the door.

The club meeting was held in the Izaak Walton Building in the park down by the river. It was a long log shelter house with lots of big screened windows and a stone fireplace at one end. When we arrived, there were six or seven families there already. The young kids were outside, chasing each other around through the woods. Their parents were inside, standing around in clots, talking. A few of the more curious—or maybe hungry—peered into the dishes that were gathering on the serving table.

The only other person there who was our age was Denny Hoffrider. He was a year behind us in school but only because he'd missed a year when he had rheumatic fever, so he was within datable range. I don't know who makes up these rules, in fact no one ever actually talks about them, but they are very real, nevertheless. If you go out with a boy who's younger than you, or one who gets bad grades, or flunked at any time, or one who is a lot shorter than you, or has horrible breath or horrible skin or body odor, then

Flowers of Anger

you're just saying to the world that you are desperate and will go out with anybody. Once you do that, no good guy will ask you out for fear of losing his own status. If you date somebody from another town, though, that's a big plus in your favor, and the farther away, the better. I suppose the theory is that you're such a great catch that your fame has spread all the way to wherever he lives. Actually all it takes is a cousin in the other school, or a friend who moved there.

Boys seem to have a similar system of laws. For instance, I'm not really datable because I'm kind of tall and heavy-boned and not exactly a clinging vine type. I hear comments about my being busty; but those comments would not inspire me to go out with the fellow who was making them, even if he did ask me, which none of them ever do.

Anyway, as I said, Denny Hoffrider was there. He was nice. He lived on a farm and his folks raised purebred Angus, like Uncle Vern, and Quarter horses. So he had a little more status than some of the farm kids who lived on crummy places. Denny was just homely enough not to be scary, but not so homely that he wasn't a good catch. The only thing I had against him was that for some reason he made me feel guilty every time I saw him.

I had done another one of my dumb things one time last summer. It really was a stupid thing to do. When Ann and I first started coming to saddle club, Denny was interested in Ann. He didn't exactly sweep her off her feet on his white charger, but he kept looking at her and sort of following us around without actually appearing to be following us. If we went outside the shelter house, he'd come out in a few minutes and start fiddling around under the hood of his pickup. If Ann said anything to him, he'd get kind of red and pleased-looking.

After this had been going on most of the summer, he got me off alone one night after the meeting and started asking questions like, is Ann going with anybody. Subtle things like that. I knew Ann liked him. I knew she was hoping he'd ask her to the Future Farmers of America hayride. I knew she knew he was working up to asking her for a date. So what did I do? I told him she was in love with this guy from Fort Dodge, whom I made up entirely out of my head. I didn't say she was dating him because that would be easy enough to check up on. But I figured he wouldn't risk asking her out and getting turned down. He was too sensitive for that.

So what kind of a friend does that make me? Right. A rotten friend. I don't know why I did it. It wasn't that I didn't want her to start dating before I did.

Was it?

All through the supper people kept leaning across the table toward Ann and telling her how sorry they were about Nipper. The first time or two her eyes puddled up, but after that she was okay. She didn't talk much, though. Hershal came over and asked her when the heck she was coming out to look at his colts, and she just changed the subject.

The main item of the business meeting was making final plans for the trail ride at the end of the month. Mrs. Paris, who was ride chairman, got up. "Our July ride will be held at Hoffriders', as you know. We start at nine, take the same route as we did last year, circle back to Hoffriders' for a picnic lunch, and those that are up to it will go on after lunch and do the upper half of the ride, around the trout hatchery and up Brush Creek and back around. That last half of the ride takes a good four hours, as I recall." There were laughs and groans from others who remembered last year's ride. "So be forewarned. Now. We need to know who needs transportation. Hershal's truck can take— what, twelve horses, Hersh? So if you need a lift, make arrangements with Hersh or let me know. The next thing we need is a lunch chairman, and I would like to appoint Ann Johnston."

I grinned at Ann, expecting her to be pleased. It was the first time they had entrusted either of us to head up a whole committee. But her face showed no expression.

"I don't think I'll be going," she said.

There was a soft chorus of, "Oh sure, you're going." "Come on, Annie, we can't have a trail ride without you." "You are too going, now don't argue."

She just shook her head.

Denny said, "We've got plenty of horses out there that need riding. You're welcome to use any of them."

Hershal offered her the use of Dixie, a fat little half-Welsh pinto that was famous for her rocking-chair gaits. Ann just shook her head, although she loved to ride Dixie. Others offered and argued, but eventually Hershal's wife was appointed lunch chairman and the meeting went on. I could have kicked Ann.

Instead, I decided on a plan of action that I hoped would cheer her up and, at the same time, relieve me of some old guilt. After the business meeting, when Ann disappeared into the ladies room, I sidled up to Denny and said, "Come outside a minute, will you? I want to talk to you about something."

He looked surprised but followed along. We went out and found a private place at the back of his pickup, away from where the little kids were horsing around. The tailgate was down, so we hoisted ourselves and sat side by side, swinging our feet.

"I don't have much time," I said. "Ann's going to be looking for me in a minute, so I'll be brief. First, it's confession time. I told you a whopper, that time last summer, when you asked me if Ann was going with anyone. I just made all that up, and don't ask me why, except I was probably jealous. Are you still interested in her, quick, yes or no?"

He looked taken aback. "You don't mess around, do you?"

"Yes or no, Denny?"

"Yeah, I guess so. Yes."

"Good. Then would you please ask her for a date? She likes you. She has for a long time. She's been so down, ever since Nipper died, that I think it's going to take something drastic to cheer her up."

"And I'm something drastic, huh?"

Denny has a nice sense of humor, for a boy.

"Right. Will you? And maybe you can talk her into going on the trail ride. Okay?"

He scratched his head. "Uh, yeah. I'll try."

"But don't be obvious, and for God's sake don't let her know it was my idea. I've got to get back in there. She'll be looking for me. Thanks, Denny. You're a prince among men."

Driving home, Ann curled silently in her corner of the car seat with the casserole dish on her lap. The radio was on but turned down too low to do anyone

Flowers of Anger

any good; this was our established compromise between my need for having the radio on at all times and her dislike for talking over it. But tonight she was so distant I probably could have had the radio on full blast without argument.

When I started to turn in at her corner, she said, "No, go up a block, will you? Go around past Greenawalts'."

I raised my eyebrows at her, but she was gazing off out the window.

"Stop here a minute," she said when we'd rounded the corner. I slowed the car to a stop but left the motor running. I didn't like stopping there.

We were a couple of houses down from George Greenawalt's house. It was a big place, like most of them on this block—big porches, bay windows, and a round corner tower. What set his house apart from the others, literally, was the size of the lawn, which was three lots wide. The house and the garage, which was really a small barn, and the vegetable garden took up most of the middle lot. The lot on the far side was lawn surrounded by huge dark lilac hedges. They halfhid a cement fish pond and one of those great big swings, made out of slats of wood, like two benches facing each other with a tentlike framework up over the top.

The third lot, closest to where we were parked, was George's rose garden. It had a hedge of roses all around it, little gravel paths going around in circles, and some tree roses that grew as tall as I was. It was a hot, still night. I could smell the roses, even this far away. They perfumed the whole block.

I glanced at Ann. She was staring at his house.

"I wonder," she said softly. "I wonder if he feels

anything at all about what he did. Is he sorry? Does he have bad dreams about it? Does he feel—justified—because he was protecting his garden?"

"For heaven's sake, Annie, what difference does it make?"

She turned on me. "It makes a lot of difference."

"I don't see why, and I wish you'd get your mind on something more cheerful. Like the trail ride. Go on it, will you?"

"I wonder what he told his mother about it?"

"Who? Are you back on George again? How should I know what he told his mother? Look, can we go now? I feel stupid sitting here like this."

"Oh. Yeah. Sure."

I let her out at her driveway, but I didn't go in with her. I'd had about as much of her cheer as I could take for one evening. All the way home I hoped Denny would call her. Soon.

SIX

Ann remained stubbornly indifferent to my prodding about the trail ride, and in the end neither of us went. She said it wouldn't be any fun without Nipper, and I decided it wouldn't be any fun without Ann. So I spent Sunday morning in the church basement where I spend all my Sunday mornings except for horse show or trail ride days.

I sat in the middle of the nursery room and refereed bratty kids and tickled babies and tried to keep everyone quiet so they wouldn't disturb the services going on upstairs. It was a mildly fun job. Usually I enjoyed it, but that Sunday I wasn't in one of my better moods. When one of the little boys came over to me with an angry look on his face and said, "Kevin pushed me," I almost said good for Kevin.

"Why did Kevin push you?" I asked, patiently, not really caring.

" 'Cause he pushed me first," Kevin chimed in.

"Vengeance is mine. I shall repay, sayeth the Lord."

They both looked at me oddly. I looked at myself oddly. I didn't usually go around quoting from the Bible, but that one had been playing a refrain in my head the past week or so. From little things Ann said, from the way she gazed off toward Greenawalts' house,

I was beginning to have an uncomfortable feeling about her.

I sat beside the crib and let the Petersons' baby pull my fingers apart, listening to the muted sound of Reverend Burns's voice as he wound toward the end of the sermon.

When you have a problem you're supposed to talk it over with your parents, teachers, or your minister, or so I've been told all my life. I had never known anyone who actually discussed her problems with a teacher or minister, and offhand I couldn't envision myself sitting down with any of my teachers and talking about anything as personal as Ann's depression, but Reverend Burns might be a possibility.

No, I decided. Things were bound to start easing up before long. What would he think of me? Maybe that I was being silly.

It took a long time after the service was over for all the mothers to get their kids picked up so I could close the nursery. My mom and dad came downstairs and waited for me, and then the three of us drove out to the Shamrock for dinner. This was a family tradition that my folks had been trying to establish, I think as a sort of bribe to get the younger kids to go to church. If you didn't go to church, you didn't get to go out for dinner either. None of them took the bait. So, most Sundays, it was just the three of us, which was fine with me. It gave me an hour or so every week in which to be an only child.

It was also about the only time I ever saw my dad, especially since I had started working nights. We never seemed to be at home, or awake, at the same time. He was a timekeeper for the Rock Island Railroad, which hardly ever ran anymore. He's a nice man, short, very

Flowers of Anger

homely, with a little scar that runs up and down between his eyebrows and makes a permanent frown, so you think he's always crabby till you get to know him.

It was usually the same after-church crowd every Sunday at the Shamrock. Sometimes George and his little old dried-up mother were there, sometimes not. That day they were.

My dad saw me looking at George over my menu.

"How's Ann, these days?" he asked in a quiet voice.

"Same." I shook my head. "I sure thought she'd have snapped out of it by now, even loving Nipper as much as she did. I don't know."

Dad nodded sympathetically and turned back to his menu.

"Chicken dinner?"

"I guess."

When we got home I changed clothes and went over to Ann's. She was sitting on the back porch steps.

"What's up?" I said, dropping down beside her.

"Does anything look like it's up?"

I shrugged. It was going to be one of those conversations. "Where's your folks?"

"They drove Mike to school. Something about signing up for dorm rooms for next semester. Oh. Something is up. I've got something to show you."

She went into the house and came back a minute later. "Look what came in the mail yesterday."

Into my lap fluttered a check. It was for four hundred dollars, made out to Ann, from George N. Greenawalt.

"That's Nipper," she said bitterly.

"They settled out of court, then?"

She nodded and sat down with her back against the railing post.

"Good," I said, knowing better.

"Good, my foot. I wanted it to be a trial, damn it. I wanted everybody to know what he did to me."

I waved the check. "But he's admitting his guilt, if you can call it guilt. He wouldn't have paid this if he wasn't guilty. What more do you want?"

Ann shook her head and got that look she gets sometimes when the emotions are piling up so strongly that she can't sort them into words.

Finally she said, slowly, "That check was too easy, Carey. All he had to do was subtract a few hundred dollars from his checking account, and he's got plenty of money. It didn't—hurt—him, in any way, to pay me that money."

I stared at her till she looked up at me. "Andy, do you want to hurt him?"

Her eyes brimmed.

"Yes."

"But why?"

She shook her head.

"For revenge?"

She didn't answer.

"Well, it's a dumb thought if you ask me, and there's nothing you could do to him anyhow, so let's talk about something else."

"I am going to get back at him," she said.

"Oh, come on. How?"

"I don't know yet, but I've been thinking about it ever since the check came, and I've made up my mind. I'm going to do something to him. I want him to lose something that he loves as much as I loved Nip."

"Ann!" The ugliness of her mind repelled me.

Flowers of Anger

"I mean it, Carey. I don't know what it's going to be, but I'll do something. And I'm going to need your help."

"Oh, no, you're not. You're not getting me into anything like that. It's a repulsive idea, and I'm most certainly not going to help you."

"The first thing I need to do," she went on, "is to find out as much as I can about George, like is there a hidden scandal in his past, or an old love affair, or whatever. I need to know what means the most to him, so I'll know where to strike."

"Ann, you're crazy. You're talking like a crazy person. Cut it out, will you?"

"The only things I know about him so far are, let's see, he's the county clerk, he's never been married, lives with his mother, loves his garden and his roses, goes to the Legion Hall every Thursday night—"

"Stops at the root beer stand afterwards for a half-gallon of root beer," I said without thinking. "Now look. You've got me playing your silly games."

She smiled her old warm twinkly smile at me and for a minute it was as though we were kids again, plotting a raid on George's strawberry bed.

She went on, in a businesslike tone. "I thought about getting him fired from his job, you know, making up some kind of juicy rumor and getting him fired, but for all I know he might not even like his job, so that wouldn't be any good. I really need to get started with the investigating before I make up my mind about the next step."

In spite of myself I began to fall in with her. It was habit. For the past five years Ann had thought up things to do, and I had done them. She was the one who got us started riding Nip and Sarge around the edge of the cornfield behind the drive-in theater and watching the shows free. She even figured out that we could hear the sound if we got behind an empty parking place, climbed over the fence and turned up the volume on the speaker, and got back over the fence and into the tall corn without being caught.

But that, and swiping strawberries, was about as illegal as we'd ever gotten, and I had an uncomfortable feeling that whatever she was cooking up for George was going to be worse than a few strawberries. On the other hand, it occurred to me that if I went along with her I might be able to keep things at least halfway under control, whereas if I washed my hands of the whole thing she would surely shut me off, and do it alone.

She was talking. ". . . need to go around and interview people who know him, like the detectives do on TV, but without anyone realizing they're being pumped. So I'll need your help because people might be suspicious if I start asking questions, and especially later, after I do whatever I'm going to do."

"You don't think people would be suspicious of your very best friend asking questions about George?"

"Come on, Carey. Don't fight me. I need you."

Even though I didn't realize it at the time, she sure knew how to manipulate me.

"Isn't that woman who works in the county clerk's office some relative of yours?" she asked.

I nodded. "Marian Arbogast, but she's not a very close relative. My mother's cousin, I think. I don't know her well enough to start up a conversation with her, though."

"Yes, but she's important. I thought I'd ask Brett Baker. He's been the paper boy on that block for a

Flowers of Anger

couple of years, and he's too young to know he's being pumped. And then I thought I might be able to get something out of one or two of the neighbors, if you'd take Marian Arbogast. You will, won't you? Just sort of work into it naturally, find out anything you can about him. Okay?"

I scowled at her, blew my hair off my forehead, and sighed, "What are friends for."

She reached around and actually gave me a hug, which she had never done in her life before.

Aunt Mary, bless her little chubby heart, solved the problem of getting to Marian Arbogast without seeming obvious. I went out Sunday evening to say hi to Sarge, and Aunt Mary was flitting around the kitchen getting ready for a Tupperware party she was giving the next night. I asked who all was coming and, among others, she said Marian Arbogast.

"Could I come, too?" I asked.

She looked at me quizzically for just a flash, then said, "Sure, dear. We'd love to have you. I didn't think you were interested in housewares or I'd have sent you an invitation, but then I guess it is time for you to start on your hope chest." She smiled with that coy look that "hope chest" always seems to bring on in older people.

"Yeah. My hope chest."

I had to switch working nights with one of the other carhops, but it was no big problem. At seven-thirty sharp the next night, I was sitting in a corner of Aunt Mary's sofa, wearing a dress and wondering how I'd gotten myself into this. As luck would have it, Marian got there early, too, and she and I were alone for several minutes while Aunt Mary and the Tupperware saleslady set up the table with the display on it. I figured I'd better get right into it while I had the chance, so I said, "How's your boss been, lately?" Clever, subtle me.

"Fine. Why do you ask?" She looked at me as though I'd led off with "How's your love life?" Marian Arbogast was probably in her early forties with her black and grey striped hair and sort of dumpy shape. Nobody you would notice, but nice enough, I guess. She was a secretary or clerk or something in the county clerk's office in the courthouse.

I shrugged. "I just wondered. That deal about his shooting the horse. I just wondered if people were giving him a hard time about it, or anything."

"Not to his face, of course," she said, warming to the subject, "but from the talk around, people don't like what he did very much."

I should hope to kiss a pregnant duck, I said to myself. "What kind of man is he, anyway? I mean, what kind of person would do something like that, do you think?"

She started pleating her dress. "He's a lonely person, I think, I mean just living there with his mother, year after year."

"He never got married?"

She shook her head.

"No old romances, broken hearts in his past, no tragic love affair where she left him waiting at the church?"

"None that I know of, and I've worked with George for nineteen years."

I almost asked if she'd ever had a thing going with him, but I caught myself in time. "Doesn't he love anything?"

Flowers of Anger

She thought for a minute. "Just that flower garden. That's the only thing that really makes him light up when he talks about it. I can still remember how excited he was when he had a chance to buy that empty lot by his house, oh, must have been eleven, twelve years ago. 'Marian,' he said to me, 'Marian, I'm going to have something I've wanted all my life, an honest to goodness formal rose garden, like in the old country,' and for months after that he'd bring magazine pictures and drawings to the office, of beautiful rich-people's gardens. Some of the others in the office used to make fun of him behind his back, about his delusions of grandeur, as they said. But, I don't know, I found myself getting kind of excited along with him. He seemed to have such a dull existence, and if he wanted to make himself a little piece of the good life, as he called it, why not?"

"What old country?" I asked.

"What?"

"You said he said 'like in the old country.' Did he come from some other country?"

"Came from Hamilton County, Iowa, just like everybody else around here."

Other people started coming for the party. Aunt Mary called me into the kitchen to help with the coffee and little dessert cakes, so that was the end of the pumping. My mind was in a state of confusion, but I didn't have time to think, because the Tupperware lady, who was fakily cheerful, got us started playing word games that I thought I had outgrown in seventh grade. But everyone else giggled and played for all they were worth, so I went along with them. After all, they were my elders and betters, and quite possibly my future—these middle-aged housewives.

Then the sales pitch started, and I was free to sit back and think my own thoughts while the Tupperware lady went through every single item on the sample table and explained why each one was vital to our happiness and well-being.

I thought about George bringing magazine pictures of his dream garden to work and showing them around, and having people make fun of him behind his back.

I thought about his garden, what I'd seen of it over the hedge, and how it really did have that sort of "old world" atmosphere, as though it belonged next to an old English country manor.

I thought about how few people I'd ever known actually had gardens, in his sense of the word. None, in fact. People around here have a row of peonies along the driveway, maybe a row or two of marigolds in front of the house, and possibly a patch of sweet corn, green beans, and a few Big Boy tomato plants by the garage. That's a garden, too, in its own way, I suppose, but not a *garden*.

Long before the Tupperware lady showed us how to fill out our order blanks, I knew that the garden was George Greenawalt's tender spot, and that Ann wasn't going to find it out from me.

"I couldn't find out much of anything," I told Ann the next morning. We were in her room, with Eddie Arnold on the stereo in case her mother woke up and overheard us. "I'll tell you one thing, though. For your birthday you're going to get a deviled egg dish and a set of gelatin molds. That was the least I could get away with ordering, and after an evening with those women I've decided I'm never going to be a housewife, so I'll have no use for a deviled egg dish. I hope

Flowers of Anger

you appreciate the fact that I wouldn't have gone through one of those parties for anyone else but you."

Ann was still in her pajamas and uncombed. She sat like a skinny, red-headed vulture on the foot of her bed, which was unmade. She gave me the feeling that she had been sitting there plotting her sick little plots for hours.

She demanded, "Tell me everything she said, and everything you said, and everything she said. It might give me a clue you missed."

I made up some dialogue that more or less followed the first part of Marian's conversation. She sat and pondered for a while.

"Maybe we could start a rumor about him and Marian," she said.

"Oh, come on, Ann. In the first place that's a rotten idea, and in the second place, well, it's a rotten idea."

She sighed. "It probably wouldn't do the trick anyhow. I want to get him where he lives. Where it will really make him bleed. I talked to the paper boy, but he didn't know anything, he's so stupid. Darn. I don't know what else to do. On the TV shows they always come up with something when they start asking questions."

We sat without talking for so long that I began to hope she was going to give up on the whole dumb thing.

But she said, "I guess we'll have to go with the original idea, and wreck his garden."

"Ann!"

She honestly shocked me. Her voice belonged to somebody I didn't know—and wouldn't like.

She lifted her face and looked at me. "I'm going to do it, Care. I have to get back at him for Nipper. I don't care what you say, I'm not going to change my mind. I'm not sure yet just exactly how I'm going to do it, but I'll work that out. You'll have to help me. We can set up a watch on his house, you know, time when he goes to bed, when he's away from home, things like that. It'll be fun."

Her face took on a closed look.

"Fun!" I objected.

"I didn't mean that. I don't know why I said that. I guess I meant it will make me feel better, to get even with him. You understand how I feel, don't you Carey?"

Her face was pleading with me. I wanted to cry for her. I hated what she was doing, but she was still my Annie.

I closed my eyes so I wouldn't have to look at her, and set my face so it wouldn't leak any emotions, but I listened to her plans.

SEVEN

On the next saddle club meeting night Ann refused to go at all. None of my arguments would move her off her vulture-perch on the foot of her bed. Finally I said, "To heck with you, I'm not going to miss saddle club," and went without her.

I felt naked, being there alone. There was no one to whisper and giggle with during the dull parts of the business meeting. Only a few people asked about Ann, and no one seemed very surprised that she wasn't there.

Hershal did ask me when me and my sidekick were coming out to look at his colts. He liked to say things like "sidekick." I suppose it was part of his cowboy act. He was actually a used car salesman.

I shook my head and sighed. "I don't know, Hersh. I've been trying and trying to get her to see the colts, but she keeps saying 'It wouldn't be Nipper.' I honestly don't know how to argue that point. I'll keep trying, though. She needs another horse in the worst way, even though she's not admitting it."

"Well, y'all just keep hanging in there, sis."

With some difficulty I managed to corner Denny, apart from the other men. I could see some of the guys looking at us and grinning wisely, but I turned my back on them.

"Listen, Denny, I though you were going to ask Ann for a date. How come you didn't?"

He scowled at me. "I called her. Twice, for your information. The first time she said she wanted to watch something on television. The second time she didn't even bother to make up an excuse. Just said she wasn't interested. Boy, that made me feel great! I thought you said she was wanting to go out with me."

I was surprised that she had turned Denny down, and even more surprised that she hadn't told me about his calls. A few weeks before she'd have called me up if a boy that was as good a catch as Denny had made a casual remark to her in the halls at school, and we would have debated what he meant by it, and if he was working up to something.

Denny escaped back to the men, and I went home early.

The next morning, on an impulse, I walked up to the door of the parsonage, next to the church, and knocked. Mrs. Burns looked mildly surprised at my request to talk to her husband for a minute if he wasn't too busy, but she led me around the little Burnses, who were watching television from the middle of the floor, and shut me safely away in Reverend Burns's study. He appeared a few minutes later, with a bit of shaving lotion on his upper lip.

"Hi, Carey, got problems in the church nursery, do we?" He shook my hand, which was kind of surprising but nice. We sat.

"No, the nursery's fine. I'm having a little personal problem, though, and I hate to take up your time, but I sort of need somebody to talk it over with."

Flowers of Anger

His face got solemn. He looked as though he was expecting me to confess a pregnancy. "Certainly. What seems to be the problem?"

I chose my words carefully. "I have a friend who is very mad at this man who did something to her that was really terrible. So my friend wants to get even with this man and do something terrible back to him, and I've tried everything I can think of to talk her out of it, but she just has this revenge fixation."

"Are we talking about Ann Johnston?" he asked gently.

"Do ministers have privileged communication, or whatever they call it, like lawyers?"

He smiled. He was a nice looking man. Youngish. I guess probably lots of women in his church had crushes on him.

"Nothing you say will go any further."

I relaxed a little. "Yes, it's Ann. See, we've been best friends ever since we were little, and I just can't stand around and not do something while she's making herself more and more miserable, first with losing Nipper and now with this revenge idea."

"Nipper was the horse?"

"Yes, and Reverend Burns, Ann loved that horse as much as I've ever seen anybody love anybody. She got Nipper when she was a colt, and broke her herself and everything."

"That was a tragedy," he said, with sadness in his voice.

"And the worst thing about it, Ann is a good person, Reverend Burns. She's never done a thing in her whole life to deserve having her horse murdered. She's always been good-natured and likable, and there have been times when she's been so thoughtful to me. Like for instance, we met these two boys one night at the drive-in, really good-looking boys, and they wanted her to dump me and go with them. She got mad and told them off. Said if I wasn't good enough for them then she wasn't either, and I know she wanted to go with them because she was the one that started talking to them in the first place."

By the time I realized this wasn't the kind of story to be telling your minister, I was already into it.

"She sounds like a loyal friend, all right," he said.

"Yes. So my problem is how can I keep her from going through with this revenge thing, which isn't going to help anyone and will only hurt her and him? I've tried every kind of reasoning I can think of, and she won't listen."

"Hm, that is a problem."

"I keep thinking if I could just get her interested in buying another horse, that would do the trick. She got a cash settlement from Mr. Greenawalt, I don't know if you knew about that, but he paid her four hundred dollars damages, so she has the money to get a really nice horse, but she's just not interested."

He thought for a while and said, "Yes, that would seem to be the best cure."

I waited quite a while for him to say something constructive—to tell me what I should do. He didn't. Finally I said, "Well, I don't want to take up any more of your time," and left.

Rather bewildered, frustrated, and without conscious direction I started walking toward downtown.

"Well," I told myself, "so much for seeking professional help. It looks like it's going to be up to me to figure something out. My plan with Denny didn't work, talking it over with my minister didn't work. What else

Flowers of Anger

is there? My folks? No, they'd be sympathetic, but I doubt that they could help."

At the outer fringes of downtown was the big corner lot with rows of unrealistically shiny new and used cars, Renke's Auto Sales, where Hershal worked. I slowed down, thought for a minute or two, then began weaving my way among the cars. The only head in sight was Hershal's. He was leaning against the fender of a car, waiting for customers.

"Oh, hi, sis," he said when he saw me. "Has the world been treating you as well as you deserve?"

"Hi, Hersh. Are you busy?"

"Do I look busy?"

"Could I talk to you for a minute?"

"Sure. Come on in the office. We don't need to stand out here in the sun."

The little office was cluttered and dusty, but the air-conditioner made it inviting. Hersh opened two cans of pop from the machine; then we sat down, he on the corner of the desk and I on the only chair.

"I'm really getting worried about Ann," I said. "She's just not snapping out of, you know, losing Nipper, like she should have by now."

He shook his head. "She'd ought to get her another horse, like I said. That'd more than likely do it."

"That's what I keep thinking, but I can't get her to do anything about it. I've tried and tried to get her out to your place to look at your colts, and she acts like she doesn't even hear me. So I was wondering, do you suppose it would be possible for you and me to maybe bring the colts in to her house, like this afternoon or this evening? She'd have to look at them then, and that might be enough to do the trick."

He rubbed his nose and sniffed long and hard. "I'd

be glad to do that if I could, but my truck's laid up. Whole dang transmission went out on it last night. I got the boys in the shop working on it in their spare time, but it may be two, three days till it's going again. We could do it then if you want."

I almost said yes, but there was an urgency growing in me, to head off this revenge plan before it got any more of a hold on Ann than it already had. Now that I'd had the idea of bringing the colts to her, I felt that I had to do it as soon as possible. The only other plan that occurred to me was to lead one of the colts into town. Hersh's place was only a little more than a mile from the edge of town. It wouldn't be all that bad a walk.

"Are they lead-broke?" I asked him.

"Yeah, they've both been worked with a fair amount, for yearlings. Why? What did you have in mind?"

"Well, this is going to sound like a silly idea, but would you be willing to let me lead one of them into town, if I'm careful? Believe me, Hersh, I can't tell you everything that's going on with Ann, but I have a very strong feeling that something's got to be done right now."

He looked at me, and for a moment his jolly cowboy face melted into serious concern. "If you think it's that important, you go right ahead, just so you keep a good hold on the colt and watch he doesn't get spooked by kids or dogs or nothing. The boss is gone today, or else I'd run you out there. I'll call my wife, though, and let her know you're coming. The colts are in that shed back behind the barn, a little blue roan and a sorrel. You take whichever one you want. There's halters and lead ropes hanging inside the shed there."

I stood up and gave him a worried half-grin.

Flowers of Anger

"Thanks, Hershal. You're a prince."

I went home, ate a sandwich, and called Ann to make sure she'd be home all afternoon. Mom was working, so her car was out of the question. I got my rusted and outgrown bike out of the garage and set off for Hershal's.

By the time I got out there I was so hot and dusty that if I had allowed myself to think about walking all the way into town and back leading a yearling colt in the ninety-five degree heat of an Iowa summer afternoon, I probably would not have done it. So I just focused on one step at a time.

The colts stood in the dried mud of their small lot and watched my approach with interest. They were lovely. Being no judge at all of horseflesh I decided on the blue roan because she was a girl, like Nipper, and she was such a pretty color, a sort of slate blue gray with black mane and tail and a frosting of white over her rump, the beginnings of an Appaloosa blanket. Both colts seemed friendly and accustomed to being handled.

I found an old brush and curry comb in the barn and a reasonably nice looking halter and tied the colt to the fence. I brushed the caked mud off her legs, combed out her mane and tail, and brushed all the dust and dead hair out of her coat. She shone.

"Well, come on, Old Blue, guess we can't put it off any longer."

I waved to Hershal's wife watching me from the house and started off down the road toward town. At first the colt was balky and fearful, but when she got out of sight of the other horses she settled down and went along nicely beside me. She spooked a little at the first farm we passed, when the dog came rushing out at her. The dog looked nasty enough to spook me, too, but he did nothing more than make a lot of noise, and when we got past his territory he lost interest in us.

Strolling down country roads may sound idyllic, like making love in the woods, but when you get right down to it, it's not. Probably making love in the woods isn't either, I wouldn't know. But I do know about strolling down country roads. If you're going to do it, pick a road that isn't flat open and shadeless and uninteresting and made of dusty gravel that chokes you when a car goes by and pokes holes in your feet through the soles of your tennis shoes. And you could probably think of a better companion than a yearling colt who has never seen the outside world. She was a good little thing, but the responsibility of her made me nervous.

All the way to town I plotted the best way of getting from the edge of town to Ann's house. I finally decided on going up Grove Street, which marks the edge of town, for three blocks, and then down the alley between Fifth and Fourth. That would take me right to Ann's backyard.

As soon as we were in town we attracted a small following of kids on bikes. I stopped, turned to them, and said, "Hey listen, would you guys do me a favor, please? This is just a young colt and she gets scared easily, so would you stay back pretty far away from her and not make any noise? Thanks. I really appreciate it."

They didn't say anything to me, but they did stay several yards away from the colt, and they began a whispered fight about who should shut up and who was making more noise than whom. They followed for the whole three blocks to where we turned into the alley,

Flowers of Anger

and then they wafted away. I was relieved. They could have been a problem.

The colt had grown jittery. Her head was up and her ears seemed to turn in all directions at once. She moved with quick, tense steps. I talked and talked to her.

The alleys proved to be a good choice. Most of the backyards we passed were empty of life, and the occasional dogs we encountered were either tied up or fenced in.

Seven blocks to go. Six blocks. Five blocks. There was a bad moment when a guy on a motorcycle roared into the alley behind us, but I managed to get the colt out of the way into somebody's backyard. She reared when the cycle passed, but I had a hard hold on the lead rope, and I got her quieted down again. The woman who lived there was hanging out a wash. I glanced at the grass. It was a little torn where the colt had spun around.

"I'm sorry," I said to the woman in a helpless voice.

She shook her head and waved me away. "Them kids and their motorcycles. I'll take a horse any day," she said.

I answered silently, "Why couldn't you have been Ann's neighbor instead of George Greenawalt?"

We made it the rest of the way to Ann's without problems. Her mother saw me through the window, grinned, waved, and disappeared to call Ann. In a minute Ann came out.

"Where'd you get that?" she asked. There was no warmth in her voice. She glanced at the colt, then looked away.

"She's one of Hershal's colts. You wouldn't go out there to look at them, so I thought—"

"You'd bring the mountain to Mohammed, right?" Her voice sounded cool, almost angry. I looked away from her and stroked the colt's neck.

"Just look, though. Isn't she pretty?" I led her around in a small circle. "And she's got a nice temperament. She wasn't spooky at all, coming through town. She just went right along with me. Some jerk on a motorcycle almost ran us down, and it didn't phase her a bit. Well, she kind of jumped a little, but when I talked to her she settled right down again. Isn't she pretty?"

I realized I was rattling on.

Ann shrugged. "If you're so crazy about her why don't you buy her?"

"Oh, come on, Annie."

"Well? Come on yourself. You're trying to blackmail me, that's what you're doing, and you can just forget it."

"Blackmail! What the heck do you mean by that?"

"You know very well what I mean. You go through this big martyr act, leading this colt all the way into town, so then I'm supposed to have some big happy ending scene where I take one look at this colt and forget all about Nipper and—everything else—and if I don't, then I'm the ungrateful clod because you went to all that trouble, right?"

"Ann." Her mother spoke sharply from the porch. "I'm ashamed of you, talking to your best friend that way. Your only friend, I might point out. Carey went to a lot of trouble for you and I think you owe her an apology."

I was mad at Ann, and hurt, but I wasn't quite ready to give up on the idea yet. I handed her the lead rope.

Flowers of Anger

"Here, at least hold her for me, for a minute. I've got to use your bathroom."

I took as long as I could in the house, hoping that she would really look at the colt and feel close to her. But when I went back outside she just handed the lead rope back to me and started up the porch steps.

"Maybe you're afraid," I called after her in one desperate parting shot.

"Hah. Afraid of what?"

I thought quickly. "Afraid you might not do as good a job breaking this colt as you did with Nipper. Maybe that was just a lucky fluke that Nipper turned out so well, and if you try to break another colt and mess up the job then everyone at saddle club will quit going around saying, 'Ann Johnston is a natural-born horse trainer,' and all that stuff."

She just stood there shaking her head. "Oh, boy, Carey, you are so transparent. You are so unsubtle. Did you really think I was going to bite on that one?"

I grew red and furious. In all the years we had been together, that was the first time Ann had ever deliberately made me feel stupid. I had always known she was a little sharper than I was, and I'm sure she'd known it, too. But never before had she thrown it at me directly.

Stiffly I turned and led the colt away.

EIGHT

I didn't see or talk to Ann for several days after the fiasco with the colt. I was disgusted with her, angry with her, and lonesome for her the way she used to be. I simply made up my mind to leave her alone for a while. If she wanted me, she knew my phone number; but for the time being, my emotions were too tired and bruised to be exposed to any more of Ann.

So, of course, when she called Sunday afternoon and invited me to come over and stay all night, I hesitated; but I finally decided to go anyway.

I got there just before supper. Ann pulled me upstairs before I had a chance to say more than hi to her mom and dad.

"I told them we were going to the show tonight," she whispered.

"I don't want to—"

"No, I don't mean we are going to the show, I mean *I told them* we're going to the show. We have a reconnaissance job to do tonight.

"What?"

"A preliminary survey for Operation Rose Garden."

"Oh, come on, Ann. I'm not going to lie to your folks, and I'm not going to play your silly spy games

Flowers of Anger

with you. You're acting like a little kid, and you know it."

"Carey, I need you, and you said you'd help me. All we're going to do is go over there and look around in the garden and get the lay of the land. I've been watching his house, and I noticed that the past couple of Sunday nights he's taken his mother someplace in the car from about eight to ten o'clock. I think they go out to the nursing home and visit somebody out there, maybe a relative. So all we have to do is wait till they leave and it gets dark enough so the neighbors don't see us, and then we can sneak in there. Okay?"

"Just to look around, now, not to do anything," I said doubtfully.

"Cross my heart, hope to die, spit in your eye."

I couldn't help grinning at her. For once she looked eager and alive. As long as I didn't think about the vicious and destructive end, I could almost enjoy the game. Although sixteen might seem a ridiculous age at which to feel nostalgic about one's youth, that is exactly the way I was feeling that summer, a sometimes overwhelming longing to be eleven or twelve again. I wanted to spend this summer twilight running around the houses on the block, hiding in bushes, throwing tennis balls over garages. Laughing with Annie. And so I let her carry me along with this game of Hide-and-Seek.

Sunday night supper at Johnstons' was always the same: waffles with different kinds of jams, bacon, and big, crisp salads. We loaded up our TV trays in the kitchen and took them to the living room so we could watch television while we ate. We all had our traditional seats, including me, and we had traditional fights and jokes about the programs we watched. It was best in winter, when the fireplace would be going and darkness fell early. Then the evenings usually went from supper to a huge jigsaw puzzle or the Monopoly board. One winter it had been Tripoli.

We settled down with our laden trays. The dogs watched intently.

"What's the show tonight?" Mrs. Johnston asked.

"Fandango," Ann said, too quickly. "It's supposed to be very funny."

"Yeah, it was good," I said without thinking.

Ann's mother glanced at me. "You've already seen it?"

I flushed a guilty red. "Well, yes, but it's good enough to see twice."

Ann gave me a flashing glare and I lowered my head to eat. I hated this lying to her folks. All these years they had treated me exactly as one of the family, and they trusted me, and I enjoyed their liking and trust. We'd never told them any outright lies before, although naturally, we didn't ever talk about some things in front of them, like eating George's strawberries, or riding along that dangerous river-edge trail, or doing some of the things we used to do with boys in Petersons' garage when we were little.

I was very glad when supper was over. At seven-thirty we left and walked away toward town. When we got to the end of the block we stopped, looked casually back over our shoulders, then turned the corner north instead of south toward the theater. We went up half a block, then started up the alley back toward Ann's house. Trying to appear not to be looking around, we looked around. We saw no one—no one sitting on back porches or mowing lawns or working in gardens. On summer evenings around this place,

Flowers of Anger

most people sit out, but they sit on front porches or in lawn chairs in front yards so they can wave at people going by.

When we got close to the hedge around George's big garden, Ann motioned me down to a squat, and we crept up to the hedge. It was beautiful, about four feet high all the way around the whole lot, and it was covered with little yellow roses.

Up close to the hedge, I had a bit of a seizure when I looked through and saw George. He was kneeling about twenty feet away, with his back to us. There was a brick-edged flower bed in the shape of a quarter moon, and it was filled with miniature roses, perfect little plants not more than a foot tall, all blooming their hearts out. A sack of rose food lay on the grass beside George. He was sprinkling fistfuls of it around the plants and working it into the earth with his hands. I couldn't see his face, but there was tenderness in the curve of his back. In that instant I forgot all about Nipper and I grieved for what Ann was going to do to George.

I glanced at her, hoping for a softening of her face, but her eyes were bright and hard and eager.

After a few minutes George began picking some of the big roses—white ones, silvery blue, lavender, and pink roses. He cut them as carefully as a surgeon would, and he took them from here and there so that no bare places were left. Then, cradling them tenderly across his arm, he left the garden. A little while later he backed his car out of the garage, handed in his mother and the roses with equal care, and drove away.

"What now?" I whispered. This was so like the nights we had spied on George for strawberry-pilfering purposes that I kept forgetting I shouldn't be enjoying it. "It's still too light to go in there," Ann said in a low voice. "One of the neighbors might see us. So we'll hide in his loft till it gets dark."

"If it's that dark, how are we going to see anything?"

"There's a full moon tonight, or just about full."

"Well? Won't that make it light enough for neighbors to see us trespassing in there?"

"No." She waved away my logic with an airy gesture. We followed the hedge along the alley to the little barn that served as George's garage and tool shed. Then, with one more casual look up and down the backyards around us, we ducked inside. On one wall there was a crude ladder leading to the loft above. We climbed it.

The loft was empty except for some stacks of white cones for covering rosebushes in winter. It had a small round window that looked out over the rose garden. Ann sat down close to the window, which was almost at floor level, and I dropped beside her. We sat silently looking down into the garden.

"I thought about digging them up," Ann said thoughtfully, "but there are so many bushes, especially if you count that whole huge hedge. It would take forever."

"Ann," I began.

"Do you have any ideas? We have to kill every single rosebush, and we need to figure out a way to do it in no more than, say, an hour or two."

"Annie, don't," I said softly. "Those are beautiful roses down there. They're beautiful. They're alive, and what have they ever done to you? The roses, I'm talking about, not their owner."

She closed her face.

Flowers of Anger

"If you go down there and kill his garden, what good is it going to do?"

She said nothing.

"Do you realize you and I are sixteen years old, for heaven's sake? Don't you think that's just a little bit too old for this childishness? Lots of girls our age are wives and mothers already, and here we are skulking around in people's hay lofts, plotting the murder of a bunch of bushes, for crying out loud."

"I'm going to do it, Carey." She spoke firmly but quietly.

We sat for a long time without talking. Once when I glanced at her, her eyes were brimming, but the next time I looked they were dry and hard and bright again.

"Full moon, all right," I said in a musing tone. "Look how red it is."

"Blood on the moon," she said in a ten-year-old's voice. "Someone will die tonight."

I smiled. "Remember that time we were riding back to the pasture after we'd been watching the drive-in movie from the cornfield?"

She took up the memory. "And there was blood on the moon that night, too, and we got ourselves all spooked up talking about it, and watching that dumb Frankenstein movie."

"And we were going over the Boone River Bridge and you looked down and yelled, 'There's a dead body floating on the water.' The horses took off running, and I fell off, and poor old Sarge looked so surprised."

She grinned and shook her head. "I still say it looked like a dead body to me."

"It was just a log."

"Well—"

But the moment couldn't hold against the mood of

the present. She pulled back into her new separate self and left me sitting there, as alone as though she wasn't there.

The longer we sat the more nervous I got. George could come home any time. He could drive into the barn, right under us, and know somehow that we were up there, and climb up and corner us, maybe call the police—no, that would be too farfetched—but at least call our folks and tell them we'd been trespassing.

Finally Ann decided it was dark enough. She toed her way down the ladder and went across the backyard. So I followed. There was a white gate leading into the rose garden—a picture-book gate with a trellis full of climbing roses curving up over the top. I loved it.

"Keep down," Ann whispered as we went inside. We bent our knees and walked in a half-stoop so our heads wouldn't show over the top of the hedge, in case anyone passed by.

I did nothing more than follow Ann around while she studied the beds of roses. She seemed to be figuring in her head.

"I don't know what you needed me for," I whispered.

"Shhh."

The closer look showed us nothing we hadn't already seen over the top of the hedge, just flower beds, graveled walks lined with bricks, rose trees, rosebushes, rose hedges, with neatly mowed grass in between.

"Come on, Ann, let's get out of here. He could come home any time." My scalp was prickled up the whole time we were in there, and my heart was making itself felt. I knew I would never make a professional burglar.

Flowers of Anger

"Oh, okay, come on. I guess I've got what I need." She led the way back to safety. We backtracked up the alley, around the corner, and down the street toward town. When we got within sight of the theater we saw people coming out of it, enough people to indicate that the show had just ended.

'How's that for timing?" Ann said smugly.

We dusted the loft dust off each other's rears and walked slowly back to Ann's house while I, at her insistence, told her the plot of the movie in case her parents asked. When we got to her house we announced that we were home, but instead of going inside we went around to the back porch and sat on the top step. Mrs. Johnston brought us dishes of ice cream—butter brickle, which is my all-time favorite. It made me feel terrible, especially when she asked how the show was, and Ann blythly lied her way through the whole plot.

When her mother was out of earshot Ann said, "If we just cut them down, they'd grow right back again, wouldn't they?"

"Don't ask me," I said nastily, "you're the rose expert."

Thoughtfully she said, "The easiest and fastest way would be to pour something on them, something that would kill them instantly, zap, like some giant plague."

"Ann, don't you have any feelings at all about those poor flowers? How could you change so much? You've always loved flowers."

"I always loved horses, too."

"Come on."

"You should just be glad I didn't decide to shoot George, or his mother, or burn their house down or something really drastic like that."

I wrinkled my lip wryly. "Yes, I guess I should be

grateful for that. All you're going to do is a little malicious, sick vandalism that is so far beneath you that I still can't believe it's your own idea."

"Shut up and help me think. What could you pour on a plant that would kill it? It would have to be something easy to get hold of in large quantities. Think."

"To hell with you. I may not be able to stop you, but I'm sure not going to help."

"I wonder if gasoline would do it? Let me see . . . it seems like it would. And it would be simple to get. I could just take Dad's gas can and pretend I was getting gas for the mower. He's got a five-gallon can. One can might even be enough. I'd have to see how much it would take to kill one bush."

My heart dropped. Now she had the means.

"We'll have to try it out. Tonight. As soon as the folks go to bed, in case they look out a window and wonder what we're doing."

"Annie, please don't."

But of course we did. We waited several minutes after the lights went out in her parents' bedroom. Then we got the gas can out of the garage and took it to the side of the house, where five rather spindly rosebushes lived in the foot-wide strip of earth between the house and the sidewalk from the kitchen door.

I watched unhappily while Ann tipped up the can and sloshed gasoline over the end bush. She ran to put the can away, then returned to squat beside the bush, watching it. Nothing happened. I began to hope.

We waited a half hour and felt the leaves. They felt limp, supple, tired.

"Come on," I said. "Let's go to bed. . . . We'll know in the morning."

Flowers of Anger

When we came down for breakfast the next morning, the house was empty, but Mr. Johnston's head was just outside the kitchen window, looking down. Ann glanced at me.

We went outside.

"Something's wrong with this rose," her father said in a puzzled voice. "Look at it."

We looked. Only the sturdy inner branches remained upright. The leaves, the blossoms, the young green canes, all hung lifeless. Over her father's bent back, Ann smiled in triumph.

NINE

One of the other carhops was sick that week, so I had to work every night. I was glad. I got to work early and stayed late every night, sometimes sending both Marsha and Chuck home at close-up time and doing all the cleaning and counting myself. I didn't want to think about Ann, nor the dead rose by her kitchen door.

On Friday afternoon the boss was at the stand when I got there at four. He took me back into the private corner of the kitchen, which was about two square feet of space behind the grill, and gave me a nice little talk about how I was the best carhop he'd ever had. I was dependable and hard-working and I got along with the other girls, which evidently is some sort of rarity in his business. And he gave me a raise and said he sure hoped I'd work there next summer, too. It made me feel good, momentarily. Then I got to thinking about how this was supposed to have been Ann's job, and that one reason I'd wanted to succeed at it was to prove that I could do something better than she.

But that was back when I used to look up to Ann.

It was a busy Friday night. Every once in a while I had the feeling that Marsha was working up to saying something to me, but we always got busy before

Flowers of Anger

she got it out. Just before closing time Ann drove in, in her father's car. I went over, even though she was parked on Marsha's side of the building.

"Hi," I said in a level voice. I still hadn't decided which of my divergent feelings toward Annie I wanted to follow, cut her out of my life or ride it out with her till this bad time was over.

She was bright-eyed, too bright-eyed. "I came to give you a ride home," she said. "Mom had to go to work early so I took her over."

"Oh, well, okay. Thanks. It'll be about twenty minutes yet. Want something to eat?"

She ordered a root beer float. I gave the order to Marsha to deliver, since I didn't want to cut in on Marsha's territory.

When she came back from Ann's car, Marsha said, "If you want to take off early, why don't you? It's my turn to help Chuck clean up."

"No, that's okay. I'll stay." I was not looking forward to being alone with Ann. I needed more time to sort out my attitudes.

"Say, Carey," Marsha said, not quite looking at me, "do you like to bowl?"

"Yeah, I love it. Why?"

"Oh, I just wondered if you'd like to go bowling with me tomorrow afternoon. I kind of like to go, Saturday afternoon, but it's sort of boring going alone. But you're probably busy."

I looked at her for a long time, at least it must have seemed like a long time to her. Here was a perfectly nice girl whom I had come to like during these weeks of working together, and who obviously liked me and wanted to get a friendship going with me. So why didn't I just *go* bowling with her? It was such a simple situation. I loved bowling, I had nothing to do the next day, and the way things stood with Ann I should have no feelings of disloyalty in that direction. Ann had changed into someone I no longer liked, and in her consuming drive for revenge she had lost sight of me, except as a conspirator.

And yet I couldn't quite come out and flatly accept Marsha's application for best friend, which was what going bowling would lead to.

"I'm not sure if I'll have to baby-sit tomorrow afternoon, but I'll find out in the morning and call you, okay?"

The way Marsha's face lit up should have made me feel better than it did.

Ann and I were hardly out of the parking lot when she started in. "I couldn't wait to tell you," she said in a high, excited voice. "It's going to be this weekend. For sure. Mike and my folks are going to be up at his school all weekend, it's some sort of alumni thing, and getting him checked into his dorm or something like that, and they're going to stop at Uncle Clarence and Aunt Ev's on the way back Sunday, so they won't be back home till way late Sunday night."

I said nothing. She glanced at me, then went on.

"Won't that be perfect? I figured Saturday afternoon would be the ideal time to buy the gas, since everybody buys lawn mower gas on Saturday afternoons and no one will think about it. And I won't have to worry about Dad or Mike seeing all that gas in the garage Saturday night or Sunday. And then Sunday night, while George and his mother are visiting at the nursing home, that will be the time."

We parked in front of my house. Still I said nothing.

Flowers of Anger

"Do you think you could get your mom's car tomorrow afternoon?" she asked, almost breathlessly. "I thought we could go around to different gas stations, get about three or four cans full. That should be plenty. And then—"

"Ann, damn it," I flared, "I have tried and tried to get through to you, and you just don't hear me. Annie, I *hate* this. Don't you understand that simple fact? I am not going to help you in any way. It's a sick idea. It's destructive, and it makes you not one bit better than George Greenawalt."

Her mouth dropped open.

"I mean it, Ann. You think that what he did to you is terrible, right? Well it was, but what he did to you when he shot Nipper isn't half as bad as what *you* have been doing to yourself ever since. I mean it. You could have grieved for Nipper, sure, but you could have got yourself back on an even keel, you could have taken that four hundred dollars and bought that little blue colt of Hershal's, and by now you could have been happily started on training her, and learning to love her just as much as you did Nipper.

"No, don't interrupt, I'm not through yet. You have done more harm to yourself than three George Greenawalts, and now you are going to go over there and destroy a perfectly beautiful rose garden that gives pleasure to many, many people, and then you're going to hate yourself and be more unhappy, and tell more lies to your folks and other people, and you're going to end up without any friends at all."

I tried to take a deep breath and discovered I was half-crying as I talked. "In case you're not aware of the fact, you have already lost your best friend. I used to look up to you, and want to be like you, and our friendship was one of the really good, important things in my life. And now I don't even like you any more."

I got out and ran inside. I was glad my sisters were asleep when I went into our room. I couldn't have talked to them, nor explained what I was bawling about. But I lay in bed for a very long time, aching all through my body, aching in my throat.

I thought how funny it was how a person takes a best friend for granted, especially at my age. You get all wrapped up in boys, trying to meet them, trying to get them to ask you out. You don't very often stop to think that it's the girl friend and not the boyfriend who is the actual *friend*.

Right after breakfast the next morning I called Marsha and asked her what time she wanted to go bowling. Ann was no longer my other half. I was free to go bowling with whomever I chose, I said to myself.

When I hung up the phone Mom looked up from her coffee. "You going bowling this afternoon?"

"Yeah. If that's okay."

"Sure, I was just wondering why you were going with Marsha and not Ann."

"Marsha asked me."

Mom looked at me as though she knew there was more to it but didn't know whether she should ask.

"Aren't you and Ann getting along, these days?"

For an instant I thought about telling her everything, but that would have been the final disloyalty to Ann. I wasn't ready for that drastic a step. "Oh, Ann's kind of gone sour since Nipper got shot," I said, taking a half-truth, middle-of-the-road course. "She just isn't

Flowers of Anger

much interested in doing anything like bowling, these days."

Mom looked satisfied with that answer, but a bit sad. "It seems funny, you two not doing everything together, like you have since you were knee high."

I grinned. "I never was knee high."

She got up and started clearing the table. "Well, if you're going to be out galavanting this afternoon, how about helping me this morning? You can have your choice of defrosting the refrigerator or cleaning the oven. I'll be big about it."

I gave her a dry look.

All the way to the bowling alley I thought how silly it was to have spent all these years just having one friend when there were probably thirty or forty girls at school that I would have liked just as much as Ann, if I'd taken the trouble to get to know them.

Marsha and I met at the drug store corner and walked the rest of the way together. She was a bit edgy, as though the afternoon was her responsibility and if I didn't have a good time it would be her fault. We walked along trying to think of things to talk about.

With Ann there had never been a problem about things to talk about. Not once in five years could I remember a time when we had run out of something to say.

At one point in our walk a dog came out and jumped up on us, wanting to be petted. He was just a pup, you could tell, but Marsha drew back from him and muttered something about dirty paws. I gave the dog's ears an extra little rumpling and walked on, thinking about all the times Ann and I had ridden our dirty, sweaty horses bareback and come home laughing about the grimy, hairy stains on our legs. I began feeling as though the afternoon was a mistake.

It wasn't so bad, though, when we got to the bowling alley. I always responded to the smell and the racket of the place. It was a place where people had fun, loud, back-slapping fun, and the fun was in the atmosphere of the barnlike room.

Once we got started bowling I was glad I'd come. It was one of those days when my footwork and timing were perfect, and I could just about pick where I wanted the ball to go and put it there. Marsha didn't do so great, but it took me no time at all to figure out that she didn't come to the bowling alley on Saturday afternoons because she wanted to knock down wooden pins. She was constantly looking around for boys.

When we got tired of bowling I was ready to go home, but Marsha wanted to sit in the snack bar for a while, for obvious reasons. So we dawdled over conies and she talked about boys, and I listened and fiddled with the paper cover from my straw, and finally, when no male type people joined us, we left.

"So you're not going with anybody," Marsha said as we left the bowling alley and started home.

"Nope."

"Why not?"

"Well, Marsha, that's a dumb question, don't you think? Obviously, because no one ever asked me to."

She pulled back, hurt.

"I'm sorry," I sighed, "I didn't mean to snap at you."

We had stopped at an intersection, in front of the DX station. Suddenly something made me look over toward the gas pumps. Ann stood staring at me over the bent back of the attendant, who was screwing the cap onto her gas can. We didn't speak, we just looked at each other. Marsha went on talking about something, but I just looked at Ann, and she just looked at me.

I felt a sad and overwhelming guilt.

TEN

That Sunday night seemed like a nightmare. I honestly don't know why I went to Ann's alley. I knew I wasn't going to change her mind about destroying George's rose garden. I knew I couldn't stop her, and I definitely knew I wasn't going to help her. But for some reason I found it impossible not to be there.

At eight-thirty, when it was getting close to dark, I was standing behind a tree, up at the far end of the alley, and if you think that sounds dumb, believe me it felt dumb, too. I stood there peering around the tree and wondering what in the world I would say if someone I knew went by and asked me why I was standing behind that tree.

Luckily, no one went by.

After about twenty minutes I saw Ann halfway down the block, darting from behind her garage, crossing the alley, and going up to George's garage. The big five-gallon gas can glinted beside her. She ducked out of sight behind the rose hedge, and I started running toward her, quietly, on the grassy edge of the alley.

George's car was gone; his house was dark. I moved along the hedge and through the little white gate into the garden.

Ann was standing there with her back to me, looking

Flowers of Anger

down. In one hand was a tin can filled, I supposed, with gasoline. At her feet grew one of the big tea rosebushes with blossoms as big as my fist. It was one of George's blue rosebushes, the only ones I'd ever seen.

"Ann."

She jumped and spun around, terrified. Her face relaxed when she recognized me but then became guarded.

"You can't stop me," she hissed.

I went over to her. "I know I can't. I don't know why I came. Yes, I do too know. I came because I love you, Annie. I know, girls aren't supposed to say that to each other. It might mean they're queer or something. But that doesn't seem very important right now. All I know is that you are the one person in the world that I really care about, and you're the only person whose happiness is as important to me as my own is, so I guess that qualifies as love.

"When I realized I didn't like what you were turning into, I thought I could just trade you in on another friend, but I couldn't. I don't know what this has to do with anything, I just thought you should know."

I shut up. It was a stupid speech, and I don't know where it came from. I had no idea what would come out when I opened my mouth. I stood there in the quiet night, listening to the echo of my words and smelling the gasoline.

Ann stared at me, and I thought I saw some cracks in the hardness of her face. She shook her head and looked away.

Long, silent seconds passed. The fragrance of the roses weakened under the growing stench of the gasoline.

I thought she sobbed, but I wasn't sure. She raised her hand and tipped the cup and the transparent liquid streamed down and broke over the dark, shining leaves.

It took an incredibly long time for Ann to give death to each of the rosebushes. The tea roses. The hedges, the story-book rose trees, the tiny, vulnerable miniature roses in their crescent bed. When she had gone full circle and had come back to me, we were both hardened and numbed by her murders.

We stood facing each other, our faces blank, our shoulders sagging.

"There will be consequences," I said.

"Yes."

I put my arm around her shoulder; she leaned into me, with all her stiffness and her bony angles. I think she whispered, "Thank you, Carey," but I wasn't sure.

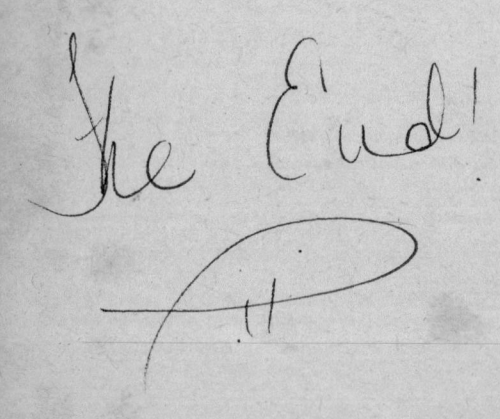